A Lot Going On Upstairs

J.S. Black

Copyright © 2021 J.S. Black

Jamilian Books — Harlan, IA
ISBN: 978-0-578-87645-0
Library of Congress Control Number: 2021906056
Title: *A Lot Going On Upstairs*
Author: J.S. Black
Digital distribution | 2021
Paperback | 2021

This is a work of fiction. The characters, names, incidents, places, and dialogue are products of the author's imagination, and are not to be construed as real.

Dedication

This book is dedicated to my parents.
Our family may be broken, but our spirits are not.

Chapter 1
Robert and Valerie

A little therapy can go a long way. That is, if you're willing to let it help you. However, Robert McEvoy lacks the will to better himself. Most twelve-year-olds do, but most twelve-year-olds aren't still wetting their beds and having ungodly night-terrors of home invasions that leave them mangled and cut open. Shadows and spotlights dance around his room while he gets lifted out of bed to be sacrificed in some kind of old Native ritual, before awakening submerged in his already-odor-filled, piss-puddled sheets. He's had no choice but to sleep in those dreadful Goodnites Pull-Ups, which are never enough to soak up his musty Great Lakes.

"Last night I had another dream that someone broke into our house and was going through my room with a flashlight," says Robert to a psychiatrist who gets paid by the hour for all the wrong reasons. "The last time that happened, stuff was actually missing from my room and we found it in my stepdad's garage, hidden away. Stuff like old toys that were given to me by my great-grandma before she died. I really think *HE'S* the one causing—"

"We're not here to talk about your stepdad, Robert," interrupts the bloated possum-weasel.

"We're here to talk about you and your problem: bed wetting. When do you think it started?"

I was LITERALLY just trying to tell you about my problem, you twatsicle.

"Well, I'm not really sure it ever started, nor stopped. I suppose it did get a lot worse when my mom left us and me and my brothers got separated," answers Robert as honestly as possible.

"Your mother has informed me that your biological father had the same problem until he was in his twenties. It seems as though you're trying to use your so-called 'stress' as the excuse instead of admitting poor genetics. I've had several meetings with your stepdad as well. He says you've been acting out and getting bad grades in school. Taking your toys away was a form of punishment he admits very unorthodox. At least he is willing to—"

Robert's mind drifts off as Paging Doctor Claude continues for another two hours about how much he likes to sniff his own farts. Bedwetting is the least of his concern. It's the weird man that his mom is currently married to. This is where protecting his mother officially began. Although he's small and unable to defend himself and her from the man, he feels he's making it better, just by being there. But the man never did lay hands on his mom. Just Robert. Swiftly behind the scenes.

Valerie loves having her baby boy back after fighting the courts for custody. Her husband, on the other hand, has despised Robert from day one. But the random physical abuse has nothing on the two years of the strange psychological abuse that has made Robert terrified of this man. He literally haunts his dreams, and then constantly puts him down for wetting the bed. *Yer mom and I don't appreciate you pissing all over the house like a fuckin baby.*

His brothers think he's making it all up, since the creep puts on a different persona when they're around.

Richard Warmurt is the creep's name. This *dick-warmer* has been waiting patiently in the driveway for his wife and stepson to return home from "therapy." Robert and Valerie pull up to see him sitting on a camping chair with a beer in one hand, and a piece of paper in the other. His bloodshot eyes glare at Robert as soon as he sees them pull in. A scar the size of a generous line of coke slashes through his genetic overbite that frowns to the point of looking like his jaw will melt away from the rest of his ugly face. Condescending smirks are all he can ever offer for a smile. His seldom laughs are audible madness (like the laughter in the background of

Pink Floyd's *Brain Damage*). Sitting smug with his horse-kicked mug in his usual faded red tank top; pudgy and bald, looking like a pissed off, bastardized version of Homer Simpson. (An absolute travesty to the Simpson name, Homer doesn't deserve such an awful comparison, but that's just kind of what he was.) Streaks of greasy brown hair down to his shoulders gather around his crowning bald spot. A fucking horseshoe mullet! The sun shot UV rays off the top of his scalp where his hair has barely ever been. Robert attempts to shield his eyes from the blinding beer-guzzling cunt before him. He thinks to himself, *What the fuck does this weirdo want now?*

Still in the car, Robert and Valerie both adjust their heads trying to get a good look at what he is holding. Robert instantly recognizes what it is and gets nervous. Hip-Hop music is his favorite thing in the world right now. He feels a deep connection to most of the lyrics he listens to and has started writing some rhymes of his own. Rhymes of an angry middle school boy.

Some of these are written boldly in Sharpie and contain such lyrics as:

My Faggot-Ass Stepdad. This and other choice words make up the piece of paper in Richard's hand.

Robert turns to his mom and says, "I'm so sorry. I wrote some things that I really shouldn't have on that paper. I never meant for him to see it. I have all my songs hidden away in my closet."

Valerie looks over at Richard with a grimace and shakes her head. "I see," she says. "Don't worry, I'll take care of this."

She rolls down her window and yells, "Hey Richard, what you got in your hand there?"

Richard stands up and stumbles toward the passenger side where Robert is sitting. Valerie jumps out of the car and jets over to Richard.

"DO YOU EVEN KNOW WHAT THIS FUCKIN PAPER EVEN SAYS??!! Richard yells.

"I COULD GIVE A SHIT LESS WHAT THAT SAYS, IT OBVIOUSLY PROVES YOU'VE BEEN SNOOPING THROUGH HIS ROOM AGAIN!" Valerie yells back.

"I FOUND THIS ON THE LIVING ROOM FLOOR!" Richard states.

Robert opens his door enough to yell, *"YOU'RE LYING! THAT WAS IN A BOX IN MY CLOSET UNDERNEATH SOME CLOTHES!"*

Richard again starts stumbling more towards Robert. Valerie yanks the back of his shirt so hard his collar rips and he falls onto his ass.

"THAT IS ENOUGH, GET YOUR SHIT AND GET THE FUCK OUT!" yells Valerie.

Robert out loud exclaims, *"YES!"*

Valerie steps over Richard to shut Robert's door. "Wait out here, Robby. I'm going to get him packed and out of our house."

Richard hilariously fumbles back onto his feet and mutters incoherent nonsense on his way to the house. Robert can hear more yelling and dysfunction inside the house but soon his mother is pulling the monster outside.

Still muttering nonsense, Richard takes his drunken-dick-breath and duffle bag, hops into his Chevy Truck, and drives away.

Robert gets out of the car and walks over to his mom. "Where's he gonna go?" he asks.

Valerie puts her arm around him and answers, "I booked him a room in town, and tomorrow I'm going to the courthouse to file for divorce. I am so sorry, Robby. I tolerated that piece of shit for far too long."

"It's fine, mom. Thank you for *finally* understanding what I've been talking about. That guy's got some kinda weird obsession with me; I could see it in his eyes. *Whatever,* though. All that matters now is he's gone."

After watching his mother finally stand up for herself and him, Robert gained an undying admiration for Valerie. It's been a few weeks since they banished the monster to a Motel 6, and Robert has been happy as a clam. His mood is especially bright on this Friday morning knowing the field trip to the museum will take up half of his school day. He runs out of bed to get dressed and makes his way to the dining room where he can hear his mom on the phone.

"Yeah, well, we'll just have to see if I'll have the time to get that done today," says Valerie. "Okay, Michelle, I'll see you when I get there. Yep, thanks. Bye."

Robert has heard her on the phone with Michelle almost every morning since she started working for R&C: A company that he has no idea about but knows she has to dress nice and sit in a cubical all day. He also knows she hates it. After ending her daily conversation, Valerie takes a seat at the dining room table, and lights a Misty 120.

"Hey there, kiddo," she exhales with smoke while noticing Robert approaching.

"Hey mom," he replies. "Talking to your friend again?!"

"She is *NOT* my friend," snaps Valerie with a squinty-eyed smirk. "We *USED TO BE* friends, but now that she's my boss I would leave her behind in an office fire!"

Robert giggles as Valerie cheeses to the point of going cross-eyed. After a good laugh, her expression becomes sincere while her eyes focus back on Robby's. "I almost forgot. While I was on the phone, I could hear that weird static you were talking about the other day. Not sure how I ever missed it, it's gotta be a recent thing!"

Robert nods his head in agreement, "Yeah! It's like a quiet, fuzzy, radio playing sports. Heard it last week when I was talking to Tommy."

Just as Valerie starts to respond she is interrupted by the ear-piercing squeal of school bus brakes. "Welp, sounds like your bus is here. I–"

"I love you, Mom," exclaims Robert as he squeezes his mother before she herself can say *I love you.*

"My goodness, I love you too, Son!" Valerie hugs back and lifts him off his feet. "Have fun at school!"

When the bus leaves, she finishes getting ready and drives to work. Mother and Son ride gallantly off to their separate destinations. Feeling so *safe*.

This museum is chock full of boob-shaped, vagina-drawn, dick-and-ball-sculpted artifacts. Robert and his buddies break from the class to discover them all. Laughing it up, goofing around, a full herd of alpha dog class clowns. These buddies were Robby's first real friends. In their quaint little suburb, they've been building forts and breaking into abandoned houses all over town. Sharing stories of their parents' porn stashes while playing Tony Hawk's Pro-Skater on the PS One. They found it fun to play carelessly with knives. Well, some of them did. Robert and his good friend, Tommy, never really cared for those games.

Robert eventually breaks away from his band of buds to look at a painting that caught his peripheral vision. It was a painting of an old woman; but her cold, dark eyes reminded him of his faggot-ass stepdad. The back of his neck tingles with peach-fuzz and he can almost hear each hair erecting. Trembling in a now cold sweat as he thinks back to when he'd sit in his room and fail miserably to play his guitar. The bald werewolf would literally howl while sitting in the living room where the doorway could reveal each other if they leaned forward just right. The first few howls and belts of laughter were somewhat amusing, but Robert, like anyone, had a boiling point. He leaned forward just enough to shut the door so he couldn't hear Richard laughing anymore. He sat back and continued to butcher Korn's *Falling Away from Me*. His eldest brother, Connor, taught him the introduction to that song.

Lost in the euphoria of what the song should sound like and the way it makes him feel, he could almost smell Connor's nicotine-coated bedroom. That is until his doorknob obnoxiously turned, and the door bounced off his wall with a loud *CRACK!* Robert practically jumped out of his skin and hid behind his cheap Yamaha. When he built up the courage to peek over his guitar's body, he saw Richard standing above him with his hand cocked back, breathing loudly.

"What's going on in there?"

Valerie's voice had barely carried into his bedroom, since she was banging dishes around in the kitchen sink with the water running.

"Oh, nuthin Val! Just little Robby droppin his guitar on the floor again!" Richard yelled back. After lowering his hand, he walked back into the living room and sat upright in his chair.

Robert had worked up the nerve to play a few more torturous bars but realized his chord had come unplugged in the confrontation. When he leaned forward to plug the cable back into the amplifier, he spotted Richard glaring at him with anger and utter distaste. *The fuckin TV's on in the living room, he's got the remote in his hand, and everything! Why the hell is he staring at me like that? Is he gonna kill me in my sleep?* That is when Robert started imagining being hung from a hook in a dirty garage and fileted from the chest down, leaving his guts to hang lower than his un-pubed pecker. From that day on, any time Robert had been in his room alone and his mother was in the kitchen, Richard Warmurt would haunt him with this thought-provoking stare. *Fuckin Dick-warmer!*

Now, so lost in thought, Robert's eyes are useless, gazing through the painting. That's when Tommy yells, "Oh shit man, there's your step-dad!!!"

Robert's heart falls into his underwear as he walks cautiously to Tommy. "Where? Where is he? *I'm not kidding man, where the fuck is he?"*

"Calm down dude. He was just talkin bout this dick-shaped Smithsonian Crystal!" Answers his friend, Kevin: the most-knife-happy-friend of them all.

"Yeah man, chill out," snaps Tommy. "You really think he would *ACTUALLY BE HERE?*"

"You guys just don't get it, do you? Guy gives me the willies!" Robert whispers loudly as he shakes off said willies. *"He's just not giving a fuck anymore! Last month he shoved me off the trailer and I gashed my head open on a log! AND THAT FUCKING STARE!!!"*

"Alright Alright Alright! We get it man, he's crazy! I'm sorry, dude, I should've known not to joke about him. I've seen that fucker's weird look." Tommy puts his arm around Robert to cheer him up. "My bad, man."

Robert lets out a big sigh of relief and smiles big. "Damn, Squeezey, you really are such a sweet little bear."

The whole pack of hyenas chuckle loudly while Tommy punches Robert on the knee. They had all stayed the night at Tommy's place a few months back when they heard his mom say *"Goodnight my Squeezey lil Bear."* That nickname sticks with him for as long as Robert can remember. Laughing and wrestling around louder and louder, the crew gets busted by their teacher. "Boys! Back with the class! The tour is almost over and *THERE WILL* be a quiz when we get back to school!"

The ride back to school promises to be the best bus ride ever!

Robert and his band of hooligans are singing the chorus line to their mutually favorite DMX song, asking all the other bus-mates how they're going to see the snake, the rat, the cat, the dog if they're livin' in the fog. Which eventually calms into a murmur of: "The fog, the fog. Livin in the fog. How you gonna see em if you livin in the fog?"

Tommy then stands up frowning with his fitted ball cap backwards, just like the lead singer of Limp Bizkit, and screams, *"I DID IT ALL FOR THE NOOKIE, COME ON! THE NOOKIE! SO YOU CAN TAKE THAT COOKIE...."*

Suddenly, the entire class begins scrambling to the side of the bus where they can see two cop cars parked outside of their school.

While Robert was having the time of his life on his field trip, Valerie was called to the school to come verify a man seen holding a rifle. But Richard had gotten away before the cops had shown up, so Valerie now sits in the principal's office frantically speaking to a policeman. "Okay? So now that we've clearly confirmed who this man is *WHY DON'T YOU GET OFF YOUR FAT ASS AND GO FIND HIM?!!?*"

"Ma'am, we notified dispatch an hour ago. They'll find him, just a matter of time."

"But, what if they don't, what if, what if they can't, what if—" Valerie fails to form her last sentence as she sobs into her palms. *My baby! It's already been a FUCKING HOUR?!*

Just when she's about to leave and go look for the bastard herself, a voice on the policeman's radio states: *SUSPECT IN CUSTODY. FOUND FIVE MILES NORTH. TAKING HIM IN FOR QUESTIONING.*

As the bus comes to a complete stop, the officer who had been patrolling the exterior of the school walks up. The bus driver pulls the handle to allow the bus doors to fold open. "What's goin on, Officer?" asks the driver.

"That's police business, sir. However, is there a *Robert McEvoy* on this bus?" The officer asks as he walks up the steps and into the bus aisle.

Robert looks around to see everybody looking at him. "Um…Present?!"

"Your mom is here to pick you up, son. Everybody make way so Robert can exit the vehicle. School hours will proceed as normal until further notice."

As Robert sits up, Tommy grabs his arm and says, "Whatever you do, don't tell them about the Rest Stop." Robert gets nervous as he remembers he and Tommy had almost burnt down their town's rest area for bicyclists along their beloved pea-gravel trail. Nearly a month ago they were setting paper towels on fire, and before they left, they were quite certain they had put everything out. Nobody got hurt and the Rest Stop still stands to this day, it was merely a smoldering trashcan that smoked enough to cause a panic for the Fire Department. Robert and Tommy still feel uneasy about that whole situation, nonetheless. Luckily for them, this police visit wasn't for their torch-lighter shenanigans, but for Robert's near extinction.

Robert gets off the bus thinking he's in deep shit, but when he sees his mom, she looks *scared* and *sad*, not angry and disappointed. "Mom, what's going on?"

"*We. Are going. To your grandmother's. TONIGHT. To live. We're going home, packing up some stuff. AND LEAVING!*" Valerie says while she hysterically bobs her head back and forth with stern hand gestures in the car.

"Why? What the hell happened?" asks Robert.

"We're not safe here, Robby. WE. ARE NOT. SAFE."

"Mom, just tell me wha—"

"*I'M NOT GONNA FUCKING TELL YOU WHAT HAPPENED! WE'RE NOT SAFE. WHAT HAPPENED AT THE SCHOOL CAN WAIT ANOTHER DAY. WE ARE LEAVING. END OF STORY!*"

"But all my friends are here, goddammit! You promised we would never move again."

"*I know, I know, Robby. I'm so sorry, baby. I would never break my promise if I knew we were safe here. You gotta trust me. We need to be strong.*"

Robert sits silently staring into the side-mirror the rest of the way home. Missing all of his friends already.

They make it home in the still early afternoon hopefully with enough time to pack and leave before dusk. They gather their clothes and a few bare necessities into trash bags and boxes. It only takes them a couple hours to get their stuff together and overfill the back of Valerie's banana-yellow 1987 Pontiac Firebird. "Wow, we may actually make it to Stanning before it gets dark!" she proclaims.

Robert stands lifeless darting his teary eyes back and forth from the Firebird to the house. *"Do you think we'll be able to come back soon?"*

"I don't know, honey. I'd love to tell you we could come back tomorrow, but... Ok, I tell ya what, I'll check in with my friend Darcy from work to see what's going on, in say, about two months. Is that okay, baby? Just think of it as a vacation, no school, no nuthin. Just you, me, Grandma, and Grandpa. You gotta be pretty excited to see Grandpa!" With this he agreed. "Also, I almost forgot, Grandma called earlier, and *YOUR BROTHERS ARE GONNA COME SEE YOU TONIGHT!!!*" Robert's whole face lights up as his mood goes from depressed to happy like a bipolar light switch. Now, rushing his mother to leave, Robert dances around the car and makes funny whistling noises. Valerie looks upon her son with a chip on her shoulder for turning her baby boy's attitude around. All set to leave, key in the ignition, motor running, heat blasting out of the dash in the late, oddly lukewarm, snow-patched winter. Thirty-two degrees felt like summer after the negative three in December. She puts the car in reverse just to put it right back into park. "What, Mom, did you forget something?"

"Yes, I did, I can't believe I almost forgot our family photos! They're up in the garage attic. How stupid of me, *CAN'T LEAVE WITHOUT THE PICTURES OF MY BABIES!!!*" Valerie's voice jokingly cries. "Can you pwease go get dem, Pookies?!" Robert hated when his mom did her baby-talk. Thank Fuck none of his friends ever heard THESE words! The bright sun reflects off the patches of snow causing temporary blindness. "Yeah, *OK*, Mom. I'll go up and get your pictures. Turn the heat down, ya goon, it ain't *THAT COLD* out there, *JEEZ!*"

Robert exits the vehicle and runs to the garage, attempting to make this as fast as possible, anxious to get to Stanning. After he opens the door to step inside, he notices the light is already on. He doesn't think too much about it, though, and makes his way to the built-in ladder that leads to the attic. Looking up through the cut-out square, he can see the light to the attic is also on. *Whatever, screw it,* thinks Robert. Climbing up swiftly, he reaches the top where half his body pokes through the square to reveal one of the most frightening scenes he's ever witnessed.

His heart is in his trousers again as he lists off the items found in the attic. A loosely made bed, a plugged-in space heater that's still running, a phone line hooked up to their hamburger phone someone got them as a gag gift, Hustler magazines, and a TV playing *Family Matters*. He doesn't even bother trying to find Mom's photos and jumps down to nearly break his ankles.

Valerie, still in the car, sees her son pale as a ghost running toward her. She gets out to meet him halfway. "What's the matter, sweetie?"

"Mom. Mom. You gotta. You gotta see. *YOU GOTTA SEE WHAT'S UP THERE!!*" Robert is so frightened he begins to cry and leaps back into the Firebird.

"Robby, what the fuck?!" Valerie yells through the car.

"Just go, Mom. *YOU HAVE TO!!!*"

Robert's whole family tree festers with bad nerves. Their genetics provide shaky hands every morning, nervous stomachaches in the afternoon, and insomnia by nightfall. Robert right now is stricken with gut-wrenching diarrhea but refuses to leave the car. His mother is starting to feel the same, *you know, it's just that right time of day!*

Valerie skeptically enters the garage, and like her unfortunate son, makes her way up to the attic. She throws up in her mouth when she gets to the top. She sees everything that Robert had seen; only she climbs all the way in to crawl on her knees around the *loveshack*. Yep, she sees the bed, the heater, the phone, the nudie magazines, and Steve Urkel on the TV. There's so much more than that, though; *something even more disturbing, vile, and incriminating.*

On the floor close to the bed sits some family photos she was looking for. Photos of her baby boy, such as school pictures and their most recent Adventureland visit. She full on vomits and nearly defecates herself as the photos are mostly stuck together near a box of Kleenex and a bottle of Strawberry-Flavored Lubricant. A fresh puddle of semen is pooled up atop Robert's Kindergarten picture. She can practically see the tiny sperm swimming around her baby's eyes. Tears pour out of her as she shakes unbearably, moaning and gagging. With her hands now making small waves as though she's massaging invisible dough, she opens a small wooden box that contains more photos.

Photos taken by Richard, for Richard, of Robert sleeping. She screams loud enough for Robert to hear, but he thankfully keeps himself planted in the car. She immediately grabs the hamburger phone to dial 911. She vomits 3 more times while on the phone with the police and relieves herself in her underwear uncontrollably. Robert finally sees his mom walking frantically with obvious shakes toward the house. He gets out to follow her inside. Seeing his mother so bent out of shape un-sewed his ass from the cloth, black and grey passenger seat. Valerie has a look in her eye the likes of which she had been in the Vietnam War and seen too many dead bodies. From that point on her eyes were forever scarred in this manner.

She wraps her arms around Robert and holds him like never before. *"I am so sorry. I can't. I can't believe how sick that man is. I just. I just. Can't.*

"I will *NEVER* let this *FUCKING SHIT HAPPEN AGAIN! I PROMISE! I PROMISE! I PROMISE, ROBBY! I PROMISE! I'M SO SORRY!"*

Robert can feel her trembling like a bad cold shiver in below zero weather. "Mom! Let's get the flyin fuck outta here, why are we even back in this stupid-ass house?"

"We'll leave, we'll leave. You bet your ass we're leavin. I gotta change my clothes. Mommy had an accident, honey. Actually, just let me change my undies and we'll get the hell outta here. I'll shower and change at Grandma's. Oh shit, I called the cops. *I called the cops.* We gotta get outta here before they get here. Had enough of their bullshit for one day." Valerie says all of this while changing her underwear quickly underneath her dress that she put on for the road trip. "Ok, let's go, let's go."

They get a block away when they see a squad car park in their driveway. Valerie stops to look back and make sure the officer goes into the garage. He does. She feels slightly better, but forever doomed with the horrible memory of those fucking pictures. "Mom, you forgot to grab the family photos," Robert says with concern. She tries so hard not to cry it boils radioactive gas in her entire midsection. "We'll make new ones, baby. We will make new ones."

About thirty minutes go by on their drive to Stanning. They've been sitting in silence with the radio hardly turned up. Valerie reaches out, shuts off the radio, grabs Robert's hand, and finally asks the unbearable question that's been bugging her since they left. "So… What all did you see up there, Robby?"

"Huh? Oh, just that the psycho was living up there! And now I know what that weird-staticky noise was on the phone. He was listening in on us, Mom! I was too scared to snoop around. Never been so weirded out in all my life. Did you find something?"

A much-needed ease falls over her as she says, "No I didn't really snoop around either, just freaked out and called the cops."

"Mom, I don't care if we ever go back there now," states Robert out of the blue, looking straight ahead, his mind lost in thought.

In the distance Robert could see the orange water tower of Rosewood from Highway 47 growing bigger and he felt a rush of nostalgia wash over him with a tingling sentimental sensation. They would head east on 33 and be in Stanning within twenty minutes. His mind swims with memories of growing up in this area in his former years, prior to all of the northern Iowa travelling and Mom's weird boyfriends/future ex-husband.

The golden days. When the family was whole.

Robert's older brothers, Douglas and Connor (Connor being the oldest), double-bouncing him on their 14-foot trampoline while trying to remain in a cannonball position in a classic game of Break the Egg. At night they'd play hide-and-go-seek on their big country lawn with the trampoline as their base, and when they grew tired, they would sleep under the stars atop their bouncy babysitter snug in their sleeping bags. Three peas in a pod. They would wake up and find that they had cuddled through the night as if they were each other's teddy bears. Robert had not been wetting the bed at that time, sparing them the Yellow River that came to be some years later.

Mom and Dad never really seemed to exist.

Financially they had been fairly well off due to a car accident that landed them both on Disability with a bonus settlement. Mom had practically broken her neck and Dad shattered four discs in his spine. They had been driving home from work together in their once-mint-condition Lincoln Continental when a Schwann's truck T-boned them on a gravel intersection. The stretch of time that his parents had been in the hospital is a blur to Robert. He had been a toddler when it happened and can only remember staying at his grandparents' trailer, and his brothers had told him that Mommy and Daddy were practically coma-toast.

His parents had been out of work for what seemed like his entire childhood. They spent most of their days locked in their room while the three boys got themselves ready for school. Connor had a school permit and drove them every day while they ate peanut-butter toast and listened to the Blues Travelers or The Dave Matthews Band. When they'd get home around 3:45, Mom and Dad would still be locked away. Every now and then they would rent movies and watch them with their kids but mostly they cared about their pills. Muscle-relaxers and Hydrocodone. But come Christmas morning their presence would not go un-noticed as they bought their children's love/respect with big expensive gifts.

Their presence especially became apparent when they decided to divorce and divide. The mutual decision worked its magic and clouded doom above the three boys with its never-ending cast of failed marriage. While their parents had been growing further and further apart; Robby, Douglas, and Connor were growing closer and closer not only as brothers, but as friends as well. By that time Connor was old enough for emancipation and moved him and Douglas to a friend's place in Cornbelt. Robert was forced to be bounced back and forth between Mom and Dad in a custody battle that had finally ended in his mom's favor only a few years ago.

Robert awoke to the car parking in his grandparents' driveway. He hadn't even known he'd been sleeping or for how long. His smile first hit his eyes and then the smirk that would one day be notorious for brightening an entire workplace formed under his flared nostrils. His happiness level off the charts with much-needed relief after such a long, bizarre day. Soon he will see his brothers.

Chapter 2
Robert and William

Connor and Douglas had not made an appearance on his first night back in Stanning. He half-expected his mother was bluffing when she told him he would see them both on such short notice. It turned out they were really planning on visiting but got busy partying with their friends instead. He didn't allow that to get to him, though, no matter how hard Valerie tried to tell him that they were inconsiderate pricks for ditching him. She had started to rant and rave about leaving the state and starting fresh elsewhere and how she had met a nice woman online from Indiana offering her and her son to come live with her. *No, you met a MAN from Indiana, is more like it,* Robert thought. It seemed to him that this whole scenario had been setup with her knowing how it would play out so she could use it to turn him against his own flesh and blood, and he would then be more apt to tag along, leaving everybody behind so she could go sleep with some dipshit stranger from AOL.com.

After all they had been through that day, Robert grew highly irritated with her. He lashed out, to his own surprise, and screamed at her: "I just wanna see my fucking Brothers! You go wherever you want! I'm staying *RIGHT HERE.*"

That tantrum earned him a solid slap across the face. She was just as exhausted by their long day as he was and irrationally hit him hard, hurting his pride more than his face. Although both were in enormous pain.

"Robby, I'm... I'm so sorry. Please..."

But her little Robby had already stormed away before she could try to apologize. He went to the spare room of the double-wide trailer, plopped face-first onto the air mattress his grandma had lain out for him, and cried with hate-filled anger. He could faintly hear Grandpa yelling at his bratty, self-righteous daughter and hoped it was making her feel as small as she had just made him feel. He had never been hit in the face by one of his parents before. Richard Warmurt had rung his bell on occasion, and if his father had known any of this was happening, he would immediately bury Sir Dick-warmer in a shallow grave and have his mom locked up in a looney bin.

I sure do miss you, Dad.

And with that being his final thought before falling fast asleep, he called his father to come pick him up the next morning.

William McEvoy was a drop-everything kind of man when it came to his sons. Especially for his

Robert. He had cleaned up his act and worked daily to better himself after the divorce. The doctors had told him he would be paralyzed within the next ten years following the car accident. Here he is, though, walking without even a limp, proving them wrong as it is nearing the "ten-year deadline." The man's a machine. He picked up a job with his uncles in their partner-owned mechanic shop. When not pulling wrenches he was pumping iron, adding pounds of muscle to his already-massive body. If you saw Robert and William standing next to each other on the street, you would never guess they were father and son. Not even uncle and nephew.

William stood at six feet tall in the eighth grade and ended at 6'4" out of high school. Robert and Connor got their height (and looks) from their mother (short and Swedish-looking). Douglas ended up being the blessed one at six feet even (tall and obviously Irish) like his father. If there was one thing William was proud of, it was Douglas's uncanny resemblance to himself. Curly red hair and tall. Connor and Robert were both short and blonde. Damn toe-heads looked too much like their mother to earn props at the dinner table such as Douglas had always obtained. Of course, their mother was smitten by all three, but she held a much softer spot for Connor and Robert.

Shortly after hanging up with his old man, he told nobody about the phone call he had made. Mostly because he was the only one awake. His grandparents, bless their hearts, have always been night-owls who catch their Zs by day. The anger he had fallen asleep with awakened with him and he could give three fucks less if his mom knows he's about to leave with his dad. He decides to wait outside and let everyone sleep.

Almost as if his father had been awaiting this phone call impatiently with the shot of redemption he must feel at having another crack at parenthood, he arrived within the hour.

"Where's your mother?" William asks as he exits his 1992 Ford Tempo. Robert had to hold back laughter at the thought of him looking like a monkey fucking a football in that small car.

"She's still asleep, but…"

"Go wake her up. You can't just walk out on her like that, I know you want to and probably flat-out need to, but you have to let her know. It wouldn't be right for us to just leave."

Robert lets out a long sigh. "Fine."

He walks back inside the trailer and is immediately hit with doubtful inner conflict of how this is all collapsing so fast. He must be out of his mind. *I can't leave my Mom, this is ridiculous.*

But that's when Valerie wakes up and stumbles out of her room to him. She had apparently tied one on after their confrontation, and was still feeling buzzed up enough to yell:

"You just want me to leave, huh? Just like that? After all the shit we've been through?"

"Mom, wait…"

"No, you listen to me, Robert." She only calls him Robert when she's mad at him. "You have no idea what I've been through trying to keep it all together for you. And it's all just blown up in my face. Sometimes I wonder if I should just leave *YOU* behind along with everyone else and maybe things will finally go my way."

"Mom, you're dru–"

"Fuck it, Robert! Fuck it!" She said the last "fuck it" loud enough to catch William's attention. He lets himself in.

"Valerie, Robert's coming with me. He needs to be away from you for a while, perhaps a nice *LONG* while."

"Oh, hey there, Mister Knight in Shining Armor, how bout one last lay? One for the road?" Valerie snickers and snorts and falls backward onto the couch that was luckily there to catch her.

"We're leavin, Val. You better come hug your son."

"Yeah whatever. Fuck it, Will. Fuck it!"

Robert gathered his stuff with tears stinging his eyes and they left Valerie behind in Grandma and Grandpa's trailer snoozing on the couch. He had glanced in at Grams and Gramps, but they were sleeping way too peacefully to be disturbed with this bucket of shit. He left without saying a proper goodbye to any of them, and that made the tears flow full-fledged all the way home to his father's place.

He was none the wiser of the toll the previous day had taken on his mother. He hadn't seen what she had seen in that awful attic. She was just beginning a losing battle with severe post-traumatic stress, and the drinking would only worsen from here.

Needless to say, Robert had left at the perfect time, regardless of the terrible way it had ended. His father's house had more than enough room to accommodate the two of them. It was equipped with a full two-room attic finished with wood-paneled walls, carpeted floors, and enough plug-ins to host a Van Halen concert. It's all Robert's now. He practically has his own apartment on the second floor. William had brought up a spare TV along with a couch from the basement so one of his two rooms functions as a living room. The other room has his bed, dresser, and a closet full of old action figures, Hot-wheels, and Lego sets from Robert's childhood/golden years that William had kept safe and sound. It is almost like a wonderful sort-of time machine, but there is so much missing. All the Stretch Armstrongs, Crash Dummies, and Ninja Turtles in the world cannot fill that void.

First of all, his brothers hadn't spoken to neither William nor Valerie since they moved out all those ages ago. That, mixed with the fact his father lives on a dead-end road in the middle of nowhere, lessens the chance of seeing them anytime soon. He feels his odds would've been better in Stanning, because they had friends and other family there that they would certainly visit with some frequency. Secondly, the home felt a little like Alcatraz, an obviously nicer version but so far away from civilization. Robert, in the travels with his mom, had become somewhat of a city boy. Solitude would take some getting used to.

While Robert was feeling all these mixed emotions, William was just thrilled to have his son back in his life. Valerie had agreed she was no longer fit as a parent and gave the exhaustedly-fought-for-custody right back to her ex-husband. Everything was unraveling in such rapid succession, neither of them could truly believe it was happening.

His father was so happy to have him back, he planned trips for the two of them to go to Adventureland in Des Moines that summer; and Minneapolis in the fall to stay with some distant relatives before attending the Vikings-Panthers game. William had been working hard and saving up little by little from each earned paycheck, which by then had accumulated quite handsomely.

They would use some savings to father-son bond like legends. And that's just what they did.

Their relationship never seemed to have the strength of Valerie's and Robby's, for reasons highly uncertain to either of them, but their love for one another was unquestionable. Both planned trips were huge successes, and they were getting very comfortable with their new lives. Hell, even Robert's new school was nice, not as nice as his previous, but he had gained some friends and had hosted a few thankfully dry sleepovers.

Aside from those sleepovers, the bed-wetting and night-terrors had never slowed. Which William found frustrating and at times Robert felt like a pissant, microscopic and good-for-nothing. His father would ask every morning if he'd had an accident and sometimes, out of embarrassment, Robert would lie through his teeth and sleep numerous nights on brown, wet sheets. The frustrations grew tremendously with the lying. William would absolutely tolerate no lies especially after the god-awful marriage he had been through with that two-faced bitch. And here was yet another thing. He bashed and defiled Valerie's name every chance he could get. Robert quickly found out that both parents, though polar opposites, were equally matched when attempting to create bad blood among the family.

The following summer there had been no trip to Adventureland but William had decided to take Robert along with him to work every day so he could sit in the office of his great-uncles' shop and listen to old farmers complain about nothing all day while they waited impatiently for their vehicles to be fixed. Robert had learned a lot of the mechanic's trade but retained none of it due to lack of interest. He wasn't sure what he wanted to be when he grew up just yet, but it certainly wasn't going to be a mechanic. Robert felt that this little nugget of truth may have been bugging his dad more than the bed-wetting. His son wasn't going to follow in his footsteps no matter how hard he pushed.

Whether William felt the same way about their shaky relationship or not, Robert will never know. He just didn't feel like he could open up and let his dad see the real Robert: the goofball, the rhyme-writer, the cig-smokin' wisenheimer. Robert loved to tell jokes. Dirty, crude jokes especially, and William was just too damned dry and old-school to share them with. (His dad certainly would not want to hear the song him and his friends had made about raping nuns.) Robert made a safe bet that it was all just in his head. Their relationship was probably fine. He was too much like his damn mother. Another popular phrase that William had used to insult his son.

He had finally allowed Robert to see his mom during the same summer as the Mechanic Bootcamp. And boy was it growing harder and harder to go back to his dad's. He would cry himself to sleep at night every time he came back from their allowed time together. He couldn't help it; he was an emotional roller-coaster, and very soon agreed whole-heartedly with his father that he really was too much like his mother. Everything was sentimental to the third power. Nothing was easy to say goodbye to, and goddammit, he hadn't seen his brothers at all on this venture. Separation anxiety coursed through his blood like a restless detective on an uncrackable case. His parents' refusal to keep their family together had done more of a number on him than either of them could ever know.

William had overheard his son crying in his room upstairs and yelled for him to come down.

"Robert!" That bold tone carried fiercely up the stairs like a James Earl Jones voice-over.

Robert made his way moodily down the steps to see that his father had tears for him, as well. *Could it be the feeling is mutual?*

"What's the matter, bud? Why aren't you happy here? What am I doing wrong?"

Those questions, all at once in that order, made Robert fall apart even more and he couldn't speak. He was fighting back the waterworks of a Fun Plex, he could barely breathe. He could only shake his head.

"You have to talk to me, bud. I can't hear what you're thinking, no matter how smart you may think I am, I'm actually quite simple. Ya need to speak up."

"I... I..." He could only choke on his own spit and continue to shake his head.

"Whatever it is, bud, you can tell me. I'm not a violent person, you know that. I sure look it, but I'm not."

"I... I... I wanna go back to living with... with Mom." He felt he had driven a dagger into his father's heart with these words and let the Fun Plex open for the season.

More tears began to well in William's eyes. He didn't speak for what felt like an hour. He seemed to only be able to shake his head just as his son had formerly done.

At last, he spoke again: "Why? Why are you so hung up on her? Her choices and her lifestyle will only hurt you, son. I can't bring myself to allow you to go down that road with her again. I can't lose you again." With that said a few tears visibly streaked his cheeks and puddled in his beard.

His father was remaining calm and trying to have a civil conversation, yet Robert had only heard with his mind's ear: *I ain't letting you leave here kiddo. You're stuck,* so get used to it!

Robert went from feeling bad to feeling angry. No longer caring how ungrateful he may sound.

"I never wanted to live here in the first place! I was confused. This place is Hell for me. I don't feel right with you and I don't think I ever will. I need my damn mom! Just LET ME GO!"

He turned to run back upstairs so he could cry in peace like he was before this dreadful conversation had to take place, but William grabbed ahold of him and embraced him with a trembling bear hug. Robert accepted and hugged back, trembling with tears of even more confusion. How had he let it get this far? Why in God's name did he just leave her behind and string this poor man before him along like he meant nothing to him? *Thanks, Dad! I'm done using you now! Can I just leave again? Perhaps for good this time?* These new feelings caused the bottle-up to end all bottle-ups. He simply locked away his "awful thoughts" of leaving him and threw away the key. There was no way he could live with himself if he left this man alone to grieve over what could've been.

That had been the first official lockdown of much-needed venting emotion. One for the chamber. Keep it down for now and die of cancer later. The cancer of the heart.

It was a historical moment for William as well. For it had been his first official ultimate guilt-trip, and oh, how successful it was! Keep him feeling sorry for now, live a long and happy life while everyone around you dies of a strange cancer.

Robert was on a roll with his new skill, too. That is until Valerie expressed mutual feelings and begged for not only forgiveness but for him and her to be together again. They had both been reduced to needing each other like a parasite longs for a host. She was talking of moving to Indiana again, only with a lot more consideration than the last time.

Robert could almost feel his arms being pulled apart and wondered if he was becoming the parent in this, dealing with two over-sized kids fighting over a new toy.

He was on the edge of insanity. Pretty heavy stuff for a thirteen-year-old. He came to the simple conclusion that while his mother's poor lifestyle choices might damage him forever, he simply just couldn't sit out in No Man's Land while his mom ventured on her own into uncharted territory. Yes, he had his mind made up. But William wasn't going to allow this, no sir. Not without a fight. They would need to be stealthy. Over several secretive phone calls, they premeditated a grand escape from Alcatraz. They would meet in the middle of the night, say 3:30 A.M., at the bottom of the desolate road in front of the damning Dead-End sign. Valerie had just traded in her outdated Firechicken for a brand-new ugly bug-looking SUV thing she couldn't seem to remember the name of. They would go from the Dead-End straight to her sister Sandy's house. Grandpa and Grandma's place would be too obvious now. She would fight for custody yet again before heading east. No matter how long that may take, she wasn't about to go to jail for kidnapping her own son.

Robert was too tired from all the scheming and hiding to feel any sort of remorse for his soon-to-be actions. It had to be done at once. Quite frankly it needed done yesterday. He was sure that the longer he stayed here, the more inside his mind he would fall, and he would be trapped in there forever playing a harmonica to his cellmate, terminal cancer.

On the 3rd day of August, William noticed Robert was in a peculiarly chipper mood. *Maybe he's finally coming around,* he thought. And if that truly was the case, it was time to talk him into participating in some sports, preferably football. But they had a couple weeks before school to talk that over. William thought it would be great for Robert to blow off some steam on the gridiron. That's where he himself had taken all of his frustrations with *his* father and tackled poor souls with Grandpa McEvoy's face pasted to them in his mind's eye, is what he will truthfully tell Robert. *That's gonna be a great talk!*

After a long day at the Mechanic Bootcamp, they headed home and held a great conversation until they reached the front door of The McEvoy

Inn & Suites: The place you loved to vacation to but dared not to settle. They had been talking about music, Robby's favorite subject, and how certain songs give them goosebumps. The good kind of goosebumps. The kind where it feels as though you've fallen onto a cloud and all your problems are far below and meaningless. The way a certain smell sparks an awesome memory; music can almost bring those smells along as if your nose had been suffering schizophrenia and put you in the front row of the memory's big-screen movie. They were listing off song names and when Robert brought up *The World I Know,* by Collective Soul, they had mutually agreed that it brought bittersweet memories of when they all lived together in the Golden Days. In fact, they simultaneously received goosebumps just talking about the song and could smell the fresh creek-water that the wind would deliver them on breezy days. That's when Robert told his father he thought he would like to be a musician. And that's when William told his son that he believed he could do whatever he put his mind to.

The talk was so damned good that Robert had forgotten all about his sneaky little plan that would take place at 3 the next morning. Once he remembered, he felt sick to his stomach and avoided his father for the rest of the night.

What the hell's wrong with me? Can I really do this to him? When 2:55 A.M. came along, he realized he could. He was not trying to be too quiet because he knew his father was a heavy sleeper. His main concern was getting the front door to open without it creaking loudly or banging it shut behind him. Those were the kinds of noises that awoke any man with Dad Ears. He turned the knob slowly and was suddenly passing over the threshold and halfway out when in his mind he heard his dad say, "You can't just walk out on her like that... It wouldn't be right to just leave." Fun Plex was threatening to open back up with all its watery goodness and while fighting it off, he brought himself back inside.

He snuck up to the doorway of his father's room and let out a loud enough sniffle he was sure his dad would wake up and see him there, fully clothed, teary-eyed, and sporting a duffel bag full of clothes and CDs. But he snored on ignorantly, and before Robert headed back to the front door to sprint outside and meet his mom by the Dead-End sign, he whispered: "I love you, Dad. I'm sorry."

Valerie was parked as planned with her lights off in her brand-new ugly bug-looking SUV thing. When he got in, she immediately went to give him a kiss and he shrugged away from her.

"Can we please just go now, Mom?" his voice was broken in sobs.

They spent the rest of 2001 at Aunt Sandy's house in what Robert now considers to be a blackout period. His memory of this time frame had disappeared as fast as it had gone by. He didn't even know where he was on 9/11. In fact, he wasn't so sure he even knew what 9/11 meant. Golden Days, I'd like you to meet your nemesis, The Dark Days. At least the Golden Days were memorable, and he really didn't mind missing this part of his life, but the fact it was all a blur when his memory had always been surprisingly strong was quite a bit unsettling. Everything before the dreaded court date in late February of '02 had just been a long black sleep.

William had put up the good fight. But on Tuesday, February 26th, 2002 he had come to understand that Iowa was a state that favored the mother. Ask any single father from Iowa, they'll tell you the same. Within only twenty-five minutes of back-and-forth banter between Robert, Valerie, William, and the attorneys; they gave full custody back to Valerie, mainly basing their decision on what Robert wanted. He had no idea he'd get to be able to decide, and Valerie and William especially seemed not to expect it.

"How would a thirteen-year-old know what's best?" William had asked repeatedly. "His mother will only drag him through Hell and back, believe me."

Whether they believed him or not, they simply did not care.

The attorneys had asked Robert a dozen times over and over if he was sure he wanted to live with his mom and every time he answered "Yes" he saw his father's heart break in his peripheral vision. It all seemed too cruel and unnecessary. And Robert was appointed captain of this S.S. Shitshow. Why did it have to be this way? *Well it's simple Robby, you're a fucking titsucker.*

When the longest twenty-five minutes of Robert's life finally came to an end, he skeptically walked over to William and let the tears flow naturally as he knew dear old Dad would be driving home to be alone again, contemplating what could've been. He held out his arms to give him a hug goodbye and William only shook his head, crossed his arms, stood up, and walked out of the courthouse. Leaving Robert to hang like a bent cross with all of his guilt and ungratefulness to ponder.

They would be leaving for Garrisville next week. Valerie had voiced her opinion with disgust of how that dirtbag William could just walk away and not hug his son goodbye.

While hearing his mom badmouth his father, just as he had heard his father badmouth his mother, Robert's mind would rewind back to the time he had tried to hug *her* goodbye and all she could say was "Fuck it, Will, Fuck it," before falling onto her ass and into drunken sleep.

Robert then coldly thought to himself that his mom and dad truly *were* meant for each other, perhaps just not in this lifetime. The evidence had been clear as day. He laughed aloud at the idea and was brought back down by the recurring thought: *You can't just leave like that. It's not right.*

He completely understood why his brothers had given up on both of them.

Ah, his brothers. That was a lovely thought. They promised him over the phone they would come stay the night with him tonight, and he was anxiously holding them to that.

Chapter 3
Joey and Jenny

A loving mother stands alone in her kitchen pondering tonight's dinner plans while tapping her fingers on the countertop. She's wearing her favorite apron that reads I GOT THE BEEF down its red and green checkered front. Her 17-year-old son, Joey, comes in from a long day in his last remaining months of high school. He broke up with his girlfriend today after discovering she had slept with his best friend, Andy. This was not an easy breakup for Joey and Jenny. They had been writing "J and J all the way" on all their lockers and desks for the last five years. Five years is quite the milestone for young, dumb love. And if he would actually take the time to hear her side of the story, he'd learn it was just a one-time drunken fluke between her and Andy, but he could care less about the details. The damage is done. Joey's wrecked. Downright devastated. He walks in numb and emotionless and tosses his keys carelessly into a random location with no attention paid.

His mom asks, "What sounds good for tonight, sweetie?"

"A protein shake is about all I can stomach, Mom," he replies. "Coach has really been on my back about our last game." Joey is using his well-known anxiety for football to mask what really happened today.

"I'm just gonna go upstairs and bench press till my biceps are solid enough for Coach Fart-Knocker to get googly-eyes over!" They both have a good laugh; Mom grabs out her ridiculously oversized blender, and everything appears to be even better than normal. While Mom plugs in her electric-bill-running-up appliance; Joey finds soap suds in the sink leftover from where she had done the dishes. He cups two handfuls and throws them at her while grinning deviously. Soon they are both running around the kitchen table, laughing madly as they get covered in small foam bubbles in a Suds War. Mom's laughing so hard, she's crying. They haven't had a Suds War since before Joey's puberty fuzzed him up in the Sixth Grade. Joey's crying so hard, he's laughing. This Suds War is the perfect distraction for him to lose his mind in disguise. *Mommy's little boy is fine. Mommy's little boy is far from heartbroken.*

Running, laughing, and crying, he breaks away from Mommy and heads up the stairs to his room that sports his bed, boom-box stereo, and all of his workout equipment. He turns his stereo on and blasts some *Woe is me! My problems are worse than yours!* angry-teen punk music. Just loud enough to keep his manic cries silent, all the while realizing that he's been betrayed by his girlfriend *AND* his lifelong friend. The thought of burying the two of them naked together in a shallow grave crosses his mind.

He finally pulls himself together enough to do some reps of bench pressing. Today he's going to go just above his max of 250 to 260, in which he lifts with no problem at all. It's either: Push it to the limit, *OR*: Think of Jenny and Andy fuck like rabbits. His mind finally finds peace and all of his focus is narrowed in on the set of six presses. But soon after he sits up, he's overwhelmed with lustful rabbits yet again. He smacks himself in the face and gets back to doing another set. This time: eight presses, but the same bad feelings come back as if they never left when he's done.

He is now stuck in this loop for what feels like hours in only a forty-five-minute period. With rage he throws a 25-pound weight across the room and it makes an impact that shakes the house.

This is the first loud, ground-shaking noise that catches his mom's attention. Protein shake in hand, his mother rushes up the stairs following the ruckus. His father, on the other hand, is passed out in front of a football game with a tallboy leaking into his lap.

"Honey, is everything okay?" she asks. Red in the face and drenched in sweat, Joey doesn't make an easy man to read.

"Yeah Mom, I'm fine. I'm just under a lot of pressure. This whole damn city is relying on me to win this game."

His mother sees that the 25-pound weight did substantial damage to some drywall, and instantly, her demeanor changes. "Well that's no reason to act like a dumbass and throw shit around like some ignorant-entitled-little-asshole. Calm down! You're about to graduate; you have a lot of good friends, and a beautiful girl who loves you almost as much as I do. You have a very bright future ahead of you and you should be proud. Don't let your so-called 'pressure' determine who you are. You're stronger than that. Why isn't Jenny here, anyway? She's usually up your ass. Have you told her how you're feeling?"

Joey stares down at the floor while trying to process everything his mom just said. There's no way in hell he's going to tell her what happened now, not after all of *THAT*. It would crush her as much as it had crushed him.

"She's working tonight, Mom. Otherwise, she would be here and I wouldn't have thrown my weight through the wall like a spoiled little bitch. I'm really sorry, Mom. I won't let this happen ever again. Just look at me, I'm shaking like a dog shittin razorblades!" Joey says with a fake smile.

"Just relax," she replies. "Drink this nasty powder crap you had me make for some reason; and, I don't know, *TWIST ONE OFF IN THE SHOWER OR SOMETHIN!*"

Joey and his mother laugh aloud. They hug, and things seem normal again.

After she leaves the room; Joey goes across the hall to the bathroom, dumps his protein shake down the toilet, and flushes it. As the sand-like chemical vortex swirls down the drain, he shuts the lid to sit down and contemplate the meaning of life.

Trees begin to cast shadows onto the bathroom window; and aside from "twisting one off", Joey decides to take Mom's advice, and have a shower. He figures a hot shower will calm his shaky nerves.

It doesn't.

In fact, he's starting to think *NOTHING* will.

He dries himself off and wraps the towel around his waist. As he wipes down the foggy mirror, he sees himself for the first time since before the big breakup. He does not like what he sees. He feels worthless and broken. With all of this being the worst hand he's ever been dealt, his emotions spiral out of control. His thoughts race and race, until the wheel stops spinning loudly to land on his final decision.

"I thought he was just working out again, got pissed off, and threw another weight across the room like before," Joey's mother sobs as she's explaining to her sister what had happened.

"I got so mad; all I did was scream at him up the stairs to 'knock it off.' I never thought to check on him again. No, instead I wait a few hours later to kiss him goodnight only to fi — "

She can't finish the sentence. She cries with exhaustion into her sister's arms outside of the funeral home where a closed casket holds her son's body.

Across the way, in the parking lot, Joey's still-drunk father is having a much harsher, yet similar conversation.

"Of all the Goddamned guns I have, he just *HAD* to choose the 12-gauge. There's *NO FUCKING HEAD* on that body in there!!!" His dad is having a mental breakdown in front of a few of his buddies. "And *WHERE WAS I?!* Fucking sleeping. Passed out like the piece-a-shit I am. It's taking everything I have not to just *JOIN HIM.*"

It's been a couple months since the funeral and mostly everything in Joey's room has been donated throughout the family. Everything, that is, that didn't have blood splattered on it. Sure, they cleaned and cleaned with their entire mite but a lot of stuff just had to be burned.

Joey's parents obviously haven't been handling this very well, turning to drugs for escape. But Heroin can only numb so much for so long, until eventually they up and leave everything behind in the middle of the night. Amongst the vast quantity of items left behind; is a dresser of Joey's. Still sitting in the same spot as when he was alive, this dresser holds the clothes he wore as well as the clothes Jenny had left there for when she stayed many nights.

A newspaper sits folded on the table in front of Jenny.

She sees something on it that catches her attention. She picks it up and reads the headline:

AUCTION TO BE HELD FOR ITEMS FROM ABANDONED HOUSE FOLLOWING TRAGIC SUICIDE

Without a suicide note, neither Joey's parents nor all uninvolved parties knew the real reason he killed himself, so Jenny upheld the lie that they were still together. Only when it came time to take something when the parents were donating, she avoided them like the plague. She carried, and still carries, a lot of un-needed guilt for Joey's death, and felt even worse for lying. So over the phone she had told his mom: "The memory of him is more than enough, it's all I need."

But after reading the news of her ex-lover's home, Jenny figures she better try to get her stuff and possibly some memorabilia before it gets spread throughout a greedy circle-jerk. She had been feeling like the worst person alive and seemed to think that this might be the remedy she needs to move on.

Desperately hoping something of his was left behind; she makes her way to his house that very night. Equipped with a big black trash bag and a crowbar, she pries her way into the abandoned home.

While inside, she's astounded by how much the house had stayed the same. She figured it would have been a giant mess, especially knowing the parents' habits. Somehow the guilt had ironically disappeared while standing in the middle of the house of hearts she had broken. She makes her way up the stairs to Joey's room and flicks the light on. Suddenly the guilt comes back worse than ever before.

Sure, the whole rest of the house was the exact way she remembered, but this room was unrecognizable. She collapses to the re-carpeted floor, braces herself using the re-painted wall, and cries until her tear ducts dry completely. *"I'M SO SORRY! I NEVER LOVED HIM! I ONLY LOVED YOU! IT WAS ALWAYS YOU! PLEASE FORGIVE ME!"*

Much like Joey in his final moments, she too is now trapped in a loop of awful emotions. Only hers are even worse. Joey didn't have guilt to deal with on top of his anger and sadness. She works herself up so fast that she almost feels a seizure coming on, much like the ones from her childhood. The seizures that the doctors swore would never come back. The thought of dying helplessly on his bedroom floor next to a small puddle of foam crosses her mind.

With some much-needed luck, she snaps out of it after seeing his dresser. She crawls across the room to it and opens a drawer. Instantly, she is hit square in the snout with Joey's scent.

She winds up opening every drawer until the dresser is left hollow and all the drawers are scattered on the floor. *"HOLY SHIT! ALL OF YOUR CLOTHES ARE STILL HERE!"* Jenny exclaims. She also of course notices some of her clothes in the mix as well.

"I CAN'T BELIEVE IT! I'VE BEEN MISSING THIS SHIRT FOR SOOO LONG!" Happier than she has been in quite some time, she rolls around atop piles of his clothes and laughs while holding all of her missing clothes. It's as though she can hear his voice saying: "It's okay, it's not your fault, I love you." (*I never once thought of you and Andy as maggot pies.*)

Jenny finally realizes that what she's doing is technically illegal, so she hurries up and gets ALL of the clothes into her trash bag. She runs home, goes to her room in the attic, tosses the bag into a corner, lays down on her bed, and gets the best sleep she has gotten since he's been gone.

Next morning, Jennifer is well rested and feels fantastic. She remembers everything from the night before and walks over to her memorabilia. Again, she ends up on the floor on top of her lover's clothes laughing and crying tears of joy. After a couple of minutes, she gets to her small stack of clothes and starts unfolding to get a closer look at them. She notices one shirt in particular that gets her all revved up and she puts it on without even thinking twice.

This was the shirt she was wearing on their last overnight stay together. She reminisces that very night as she folds his clothes and puts them on top of her dresser. In her daydream, she's sitting next to Joey who's making her laugh hysterically as he huffs and puffs and lifts, with fake anguish, two five-pound dumbbells, singing "Pump up the jam, pump it up, while yo feet aw stompin!" Quickly after he looks into her eyes and professes his love to her by smooching her rapidly all over her face and saying, "Uh-uh-uh-uh, how'd I get so wucky? Uh-uh-uh-uh," in his flawless Elmer Fudd voice. Her daydream then gets rudely awakened by her itchy back.

Suddenly, she starts feeling uncomfortable. Something is stuck to the inside of the shirt and she can't get it out. She takes it off and shakes it repeatedly. An object flies out and hits the floor. She looks down at the shirt and notices little orange dots almost like spray paint are scattered all over inside and out.

She slowly moves toward the object and starts feeling terrified as she pieces together what it is. Apparently, Joey's parents never got around to washing Jenny's clothes like they should have. Jennifer screams with blood-curdling panic and dry heaves as she discovers that she brought home a piece of her ex-boyfriend's face.

A still-bloody chunk of flesh now stains the carpet of Jennifer's bedroom floor. She begins to sink into the darkest place she has ever been, even though the sunlight is shining through her window. The moist fragment glistens as though to mock her.

That night came fast. She was frozen there, with fear, all alone in her room. (Well, sort of alone.) Her parents were out of town visiting distant relatives and weren't due back for another TEN days. The fast nightfall caused complete darkness in her room. No lights were on in any part of the house, leaving blackness so thick you could cut it with a knife. The piece of Joey's face, however, still sparkles under the moonlight.

Jenny begins to hallucinate, seeing movements in her peripheral vision. But that's not near as bad as the screams she's hearing. They sound like they're coming from another room, so she goes through the entire house only to hear it at the same volume in every room.

They are the screams of a man.

At this point Jennifer is seventy-five percent positive that she brought home Joey's tortured soul. Feeling oddly happy and frightened, in the midst of this insanity, she puts the bloody shirt back on. She premeditates getting rid of the flesh but cannot follow through. The screams continue until her mind completely snaps. She belts out a loud scream of her own in an attempt to reply and finally they stop.

Exhausted and mentally drained, she faints and falls to the floor of her room. A couple of hours pass when she's abruptly awakened by a loud bang. Much like the first bang Joey's mom heard that terrible night. Jenny's eyes open, and when they begin to focus, she realizes she fell face first onto the bloody flesh. Screaming in anger she grabs the flesh, runs downstairs, and finally gets rid of it via flushing toilet. Then she hears moaning, sniffling, sobbing noises start to surface in her bedroom. She runs back up the stairs to her room, still angry and just wanting this to end.

She almost lets out another scream until the whispering starts. It sounds like prayers being said over and over again.

Finally, silence. But Jennifer is starting to feel cold inside and out. Her head begins to spin out of control, causing a migraine from Hell and severe nausea. The man's voice comes back this time in a normal tone, and it's now obvious to her that this really is Joey. *"GOODBYE YOU FUCKING BITCH!!!"* hears Jenny.

She's shaking uncontrollably at this point, hearing loud breathing noises that eventually lead to yet another dreadful scream. All of this is followed by the second loud bang Joey's poor mother heard that night. The whole house shakes, but not near as much as Jenny's shaking. Her body is reacting violently to this trauma. Her brain gets sent into such a catatonic state that her eyes roll backward in her skull to the point of bleeding.

Jennifer dies slowly on her floor beside the small bloodstain while foaming from the mouth, drowning in bile. Her parents come home a few days later than expected to find their daughter's decomposing body in her bedroom. If only the bread factory across the street wasn't puffing mini-muffin clouds of yeast into the air, her neighbors would've been able to smell what her parents could smell.

A hellish nightmare with a teenage boy's blood at its roots, Jenny's house ends up abandoned as well.

Everybody remains ignorant to the grim details, assuming bad parenting is what led to Joey's suicide, thanks to his father's drunken outbursts at the homecoming games. The police never analyzed the blood on Jenny's floor nor the blood on her shirt; guessing it gushed from her eyeballs like the rest. Therefore, no evidence ties the two ex-lovers together. Only one person left in the entire city knows the awful truth. And he's going to be checking himself into his local psych-ward here shortly. Thoughts of blowing his head off with a shotgun have been crossing *his* mind.

Chapter 4
Robert and Valerie meet the Harpers

On the road, once and for all, on a quest so exciting that neither of them know how or what to feel. The idea of moving far away became practically mandatory on their last week in Iowa. Robert's brothers had shown up, as promised, only to prolong the guilt trip his father had bestowed upon him earlier that day. They told him how they had talked to the Old Man and how upset he was and how they had never heard him that way before. Robert simply responded with the question: *Since when do you guys care about anything but yourselves anyway?* His speech was slurring over his fourth beer. Valerie had decided to let him drink a little that night to help take his mind off what had happened. And to her displeasure, here comes her older two shithead sons, already rocking a buzz themselves, trying to make him feel bad all over again. Long-story-short, bridges were burned in a blaze of glory and there is absolutely no turning back now. The road ahead is long and mysterious and after their last week; the further away, the better.

"Mom, look, there's a Wal-Mart; can we please stop so I can get some bandanas? I'm ready for a new look!" says Robert.

Inside the Royal Blue 2001 Isuzu Rodeo, Robert sits shotgun, wearing his bandana, and looking like a pasty white version of Tupac Shakur with the knot tied to the front. He feels like a new person. Valerie can't help but giggle at her son and how silly he looks.

"Say goodbye, say goodbye to Hollywood. Say goodbye, say goodbye to Hollywood," the two of them sing aloud as they make their way down the road. Robert eventually sings the lyrics as: "Say goodbye, say goodbye to I-O-WA," exaggerating a third syllable into the word Iowa to match Hollywood. This had officially made the song Robert's favorite off his new *Eminem Show* CD. Saying goodbye to Iowa once and for all felt refreshing, yet dangerous and brave. Valerie's dance moves bring Robert to tears with laughter and they both are realizing how much fun it is to be free from their once boring lives.

A little under 10 hours later, they finally make it to Garrisville, Indiana.

"WE'RE HERE!" Robert hears his mom yell as he opens his eyes. Now sprawled across the backseat; Robert gets himself up to look out the window. What he sees is a smoggier and bigger version of what they had just left. All the grocery stores and gas stations have different names. Instead of Casey's General Stores there are

Bigfoots. This makes Robert extremely excited. Then he starts to see a bunch of people wearing bandanas similar to his own but folded in ways he has never seen before. Some of them just hang out of their pockets; others are wrapped around their wrists. He quickly takes his bandana off and tucks it into his coat. (A very wise decision.)

After getting acquainted with a few neighborhoods and landmarks, Robert and Valerie arrive at their new home. "Wow, this house is huge!" exclaims Robert. "But what the hell is that weird smell?"

Valerie looks across the street to see a bread factory. "There it is, Robby," she answers. "There's the reason for the weird smell."

Robert looks over to see a giant, smiling, orange, and yellow cartoon-style sunshine wearing thick black shades with the words: SUNNY BREAD in big red bubble lettering.

A lady's voice is heard laughing (and for a second he thought the sunshine was laughing); Robert looks back to the house and sees a woman walking out to greet them. "Hey, how was the long trip?" she asks.

"Not too bad," replies Valerie, "traffic down here is a little worse but that's all."

"Who is that?" asks a confused Robert.

"This is the friend I was telling you about, silly!" answers Valerie. She sees that her son still appears to be confused and says, "Oh, let me guess. You probably didn't believe that I had a friend here and thought we would move in with a new boyfriend. Is that it?"

Robert can only blush and say, "No, of course not, Ma." Although deep down he knows that she had read him like a book and is still certain there will be a man inside waiting for her.

"This is Christy Harper," Valerie continues. "We will be living with her and her family until we find a place of our own."

Robert grows even more excited. The idea of living in a big full house thrills him; he had gotten a taste of such chaos at his Aunt Sandy's house back in Vespa, Iowa, where he had shared a home with four younger cousins and a drunken uncle. Robert had been missing them all (besides the uncle) and was in dire need of loud drama to feel somewhat at home.

"Sweet!" he says, and without grabbing anything out of the car, he bolts for the door.

"Well, somebody seems happy to be here!" laughs Christy.

"He is," replies Valerie. "We are both very happy to be here."

As Robert makes his way into the house, he notices the first room is the kitchen. He walks straight through to find a hallway that has a bathroom to the left, a bedroom to the right, and a set of stairs that lead to the attic in the middle. After relieving himself in the bathroom, he feels comfortable enough to put his bandana back on and decides to check out the rest of his new home. He proceeds to leave the kitchen in the opposite direction and winds up in the dining room where a somewhat-older male is sitting at the table playing Solitaire with a deck of blue Bicycle cards.

Robert thinks to himself: *Oh God, this better not be Mom's new boyfriend, this fuckin guy's only 18 at best!*

"Did you seriously wear that stupid-ass bandana like that all the way here?!" asks the young man. Embarrassed and unsure of what to say, Robert lies and says, "I bought it when we got into town and didn't put it on until we got here." The young man stands up to reveal his giant 6-foot body covered in tattoos. His hair had been shaven down to his scalp in an attempt to hide his receding hairline. A big boy, indeed. Robert imagined he was more than likely called a fatass once or twice in his life, and not without consequences, because there also seemed to be more muscle than fat on this massive young man. A thin line of a chinstrap beard hugs his jaw and upper lip. (Robert thought it looked cool as hell, and later on he learned this style of a beard was what young thugs called *Playa Lines*.)

"Well, buddy, that particular color is not allowed in this house," he says. "Do you happen to have a blue one?"

Robert doesn't quite understand what is happening at this point but works up the courage to reply, "Yeah, actually, I bought a few different colors: Blue, Black, White, and Red. They came together in a pack."

"Oh ok, I see," the young man smirks and gently takes the red bandana off of Robert's head. "Please grab your blue one and try it on, if you insist on wearing a rag," laughs the young man. Robert reaches into his coat and grabs out his variety pack to unfold the blue one.

Before Robert can get the blue *rag* on his head, Christy walks in with an angry look directed toward the young man.

"Kurtis, you better not be scaring this boy with your 'gangster' bullshit," belts a furious Christy. "You remember what we talked about, don't you?"

"Yes, Mom, don't worry. I won't traumatize the poor kid just yet," replies Kurtis.

A sigh of relief falls over Robert as he now knows who this young man is and that it's not his mother's new lover.

He reaches his hand out to give Kurtis a handshake and says, "By the way, I'm Robert McEvoy."

Kurtis firmly grips Robert's hand to the point of being almost painful. "And I'm Kurtis Harper; it's really nice to finally meet you."

Kurtis loosens up and smiles big. "If I made you nervous, I'm very sorry. Truth is, you just so happen to be in the safest house in all of Garrisville. Everybody's scared of me, and they damn well should be. As long as you live in this house, I'll protect and look after you as if you're my little brother."

Robert eats up everything Kurtis Harper is telling him, having longed for a new family to which he could belong.

"Thank you," he replies. "Honestly, I feel more at home now than I ever have before."

(That was a lie, and he knew it. A big part of him was nervous. But had there ever been a time in Robert McEvoy's life that he *wasn't* nervous?)

The blue bandana now lay on the floor after the long introduction. Kurtis finds it and sits back down. He begins to fold it in a fashion Robert had never seen before. He then proceeds to gently wrap the bandana around Robert's head.

"Blue definitely looks better on you," says Kurtis. "The black and white ones are okay too, but I'm gonna have to respectfully throw your red one in the trash. I know you spent money on this, so I'll take you tomorrow to get you an even cooler blue one."

After years of not living in the same household as his brothers, Robert was more than ready for all of this. He somehow feels like he's in the right place. He and his mom had made the right decision, and after these pleasant feelings, his nerves calm.

And though he did always love the color blue, he never desired to join a gang. Frankly, the whole idea scared the hell out of him, but he knew there would be perks and benefits of being in the same house as a feared gangster.

Even on bad days inside their chaotic and overfilled home; Robert and Valerie have been at peace. The inside of this house is Old Victorian and hasn't been updated in what appears to be a century; an arrangement of modern (modern for 2002) furniture and mismatched neon-colored curtains illuminate an awkward clash of bad taste. The exterior is rough with Almond-White chipped paint on its wood-paneled siding but charming from an enthusiastic standpoint. Regardless of its roughness, this home was built like a brick shithouse; sturdy foundation and a newly reinforced roof thanks to the landlord. Six bedrooms and one bathroom make up the two-story structure. An unfinished basement contains the water heater, furnace, and laundry room. Five of the six bedrooms are currently occupied by at least two people.

There's Christy, Kurtis, and Kurtis's little sister Tabitha. Christy's older sister Jody, her boyfriend Lamar, and their two daughters: Melissa and Paige. Tiffany and Rachel also have a room but are leaving shortly after graduation. Their parents (Christy's younger sister and brother-in-law) both died at the young age of twenty-one and twenty-two in a car accident when Tiff' and Rach' were toddlers. (The mother at twenty-one had been decapitated by her seatbelt and the father at twenty-two had been thrown through the windshield and cut in half by a barbed wire fence. They had left a house-party heavily intoxicated, driving at ninety miles an hour on a backroad to lose control and die less than a mile away from their home.)

And apparently, at some point, your typical run-of-the-mill, 87-year-old-ex-prostitute with floor-nipples stepped into this mess. Either that or she came with the house. No one knows. They just keep her draped up in the scratchiest of nightgowns and call her "Aunt Myrtle." It is common knowledge throughout the house that it's a lot of fun to get drunk and listen to Aunt Myrtle's stories. Some of which are memories of her being plowed in a cotton field for room and board. Kurtis jokingly calls her *Nightgowns* and even made a small rap titled *Nightgown Nipples* that he spits when she walks out from her room every morning to make a cup of coffee. "Yer shittin!" Aunt Myrtle always shouts in her humorous old-lady voice, trying like hell to keep her dentures from falling out.

Robert and Valerie are sleeping on the couches in the living room for the time being. Robert has the option to sleep in the attic but passes on that idea with a strong Hell No.

The stairs to the attic alone are creepy. Each step makes its own distinguished noise and they all sound as though you could fall through at any given time. Once you bravely make it up the two parallel flights of hazards, you have Kurtis's room to the right. To the left is a big open storage area where Valerie and Robert have set aside a few things until they get their own room.

Christy, Kurtis, Tabitha, Jody, Lamar, Melissa, Paige, Tiff', Rach', and even Aunt Myrtle are all well aware of the ghosts in the attic. They keep this info on a strict Need-to-Know basis, mainly because they're unsure if *they* are ghosts or demons or perhaps even just one crafty and hardheaded boogeyman. Whatever *they* are, *they* have never made *their* way to any other part of the house. *They* exclusively haunt the upper-level. It wasn't until after the fourth failed exorcism they gave up on ridding their home of *them*. No one really knows how or why *they're* trapped up there, or how many of *them* there are, but Kurtis had decided to move his room up there to sleep amongst *them* and hopefully learn something from *them*.

On their third day in the Harper homestead, Valerie had asked Robert to go upstairs to retrieve her box of undergarments from the storage. This task on its own was unappealing to Robert. He hadn't yet been told of how the upstairs was haunted but felt slightly terrified on his way up the creaky stairs, nonetheless.

The time was three o'clock in the afternoon, and the sun had cut through the smog that day to allow lots of brightness throughout the entire house; yet there was Robert, feeling scared of the dark.   When he reached the top and stood between the doorway of Kurtis's room and the storage area, he saw (and somehow felt) a giant shadow swim its way up the wall in front of him and hover on the ceiling above him. He had seen and felt this before at the Henry Doorly Zoo in Omaha while in the Aquarium when a giant Sting Ray swam over top of him and then disappeared into the oceanic tunnel. Only this particular shadow had no explanation. So Robert made one up: *Must've been a car driving by.* He lit up a Marlboro Red from the pack his mom bought him and mustered up the courage to finish his mission of gathering Mom's Undies.

The sun was shining bright through the window on the storage side and beamed down on the box of undergarments. He grabbed the box, took a drag, exhaled the cowboy-killer smoke, and ran light on his feet like a ninja back to the doorway that frames above the stairs. He made it! But *what in the lied-jungle fuck is this? Rapid movement under the closed door to Kurtis's room? Why are there no sounds of footsteps? Does ninja blood run in his family too? Is Kurtis tryin to pull a fast one on me?* He opened the door. No sign of Kurtis. No closet or large piece of furniture for him to hide in or behind either. Just an array of posters on the walls and a mattress on the floor. *Wait. Kurtis left fifteen minutes ago to go daydrink with his friends. I told him 'See ya later, have a good time!' So if that wasn't Kurtis dancing behind the door, then Fuck Me Runnin!* The giant shadow went from hovering by the doorway to hovering above Robert again, and that's when the sniffling and moaning noises began to surface. The moaning was that of a male.

Not wanting but NEEDING to get back downstairs, Robert sprinted clumsily to the stairway. He had only made it about five steps down when his Zippo fell out of his pocket. Had it been any other lighter, he would have just left it behind. But this was his father's Zippo. While skeptically halting and turning to grab his lighter and face the dark doorway, moans from that of both male and female grew to loud screams that sounded muffled and far away; as if they were trapped in a box of—*Wait! Mom's Undies! They're still up there! Well, they're just gonna have to stay up there! Tuff shit, Ma!* He grabbed the Zippo and looked ahead at the black hole that may no longer be the doorway and was helpless to stop staring into it. He had that "top of the roller-coaster" feeling of hanging in midair, weightless and helpless. The black hole was as paralyzing as it was hypnotizing. And then: *SLAM!!!* The door flew shut and caused a breeze that gave him the "falling out of a roller-coaster" feeling that turned him pale and made him feel closer to death as he JUMPED down the remaining flight of *Nope, Not Today!*

It was shortly after that incident he had heard how the entire family had endured ghostly experiences in the attic.

"How the fuck can Kurtis even sleep up there?!" Robert exclaimed in Kurtis's absence.

"Oh, would ya look at him," Christy laughed, "He's hysterical! Robby, yer as pale as a gallon of milk!"

Tiff' looked over at Rach' and then back at Robert and said, "Kurtis claims to be friends with them."

Them. It suddenly dawned on him that there were even more people in this house. The kind of roommates Robert could have done without. When Kurtis came home early the next morning, Robert gave him the rundown of his new ghostly experience; for he had just lost his supernatural virginity the day before and felt the need to brag about it. They then decided to investigate the upstairs. Would the door still be shut? A flight of eight stairs lead to a landing where you have to make a hard left to go up the other flight of eight stairs that lead to the doorway to the attic. They got up to the landing, made a hard left, and "Yep the door is shut," Kurtis stated calmly. Robert, less than calm, lit up another Red with his father's Zippo, and kept his feet planted on the landing as Kurtis made his way up the remaining eight stairs.

When Kurtis reached the top, he turned the knob to the door and pushed. Robert saw that there was something keeping Kurtis from opening that door. He then saw Kurtis have to use ALL of his body weight to shove it open, and that's when Robert decided to man up and help push. Halfway through Robert's smoke they finally got the door pushed open enough for Kurtis to squeeze on through, to the other side. Robert couldn't help but notice how bright it was, all over. The sun was gloriously escaping through the half-open doorway. Then he heard Kurtis whisper, "What the fuck?!" and again found himself sacking up to join Kurtis on the other side of the door.

Whatever had slammed the door on Robert had also taken Valerie's giant headboard for her queen-sized bed and wedged it tight up under the doorknob. There were scratches lining the floor from where it had been dragged through the storeroom and up to where it was still wedged. Kurtis had to stomp the headboard into two pieces to get it unjammed from under the knob.

Poor Mom, Robert thinks, *No box of undies and NOW a broken-ass headboard.* With that in mind, he once and for all grabs the box of Mom's Undies. On their way back down the stairs, Kurtis lit himself up a smoke (one of Robert's Reds) and began to tell Robert that he had never seen *them* act this way. Robert could tell that Kurtis was thinking the same thing that he was thinking: *The living family in this house welcomes*

In the midst of all this insanity, Christy also runs her daycare on the main floor. Eleven kids, five years old and under, Monday through Friday from 6 A.M. to 5 P.M. The McEvoys had initially arrived at the Harper homestead at around 6 p.m. on a Friday; so, they had just barely missed the toddler and baby train. It wasn't until the following Monday morning that the ugly mismatched neon-colored curtains made total sense. When the kids poured into the living room and Christy dumped toys all over the floor, the bright colors brought everything together.

Christy also made sure to put up a doggy gate at the bottom of the stairs to the attic to keep the kids out and the ghosts/demons in. With so many bodies running around on the main floor, Robert and Kurtis joke of falling through and ending up in the basement atop the dirty laundry.

And with all these children playing together and laughing loudly, it made it harder to think of what could possibly fall through from upstairs.

Chapter 5

Nearly two months have passed and Robert's relationship with Kurtis has seemingly blossomed into a brotherhood. The two of them have been drinking heavily every weekend and dealing the devil's lettuce throughout the weekdays. Basically, having as much fun as possible before mid-August comes along, when Robert has to start school.

"Woah, Kurtis, what exactly is the point of all this?" asks Robert as they cross the street to get to another sidewalk. "You'll see, little buddy, it'll all make sense when we make it to this cocksucker's house," replies Kurtis.

They've walked at least twelve blocks now and Kurtis continuously looks on either side of the sidewalk as they make their way to an old rival. "I just don't get how you stepping in dog shit, on purpose, will ever make sense to me," laughs Robert.

Neither of them can keep from cracking up. They've been getting ripped out of their minds on their own supply for the last few weeks and

Robert is known to get giggly, which in turn makes Kurtis laugh hysterically. Laughing and beat-boxing, they continue onward for five more blocks.

Kurtis suddenly breaks into a rap:

"Gots-ta collect my dues, with my dookie shoes,
I got twenty-seven tatts inked with all blues,
Step ta me ya lose, see? So don't dare to choose me,
Cause I'll stomp ya stupid with my dookie shoeseys."

"Oh Shit!" Robert applauds. "That might actually be better than *Nightgown Nipples*!"

"Why thank ya, thank ya. Alright… So, go on, it's your turn now!"

"Nah man, I can't freestyle like you can. I've written some rhymes but…"

"But what?"

"They're all just raps about my mom and her asshole boyfriends. Angry raps."

"Ah, I see. Ya got any of em memorized, Slim?"

Robert giggles. "Yeah, I got this new one, thanks to you and your awesome freestyles, and you showing me them songs by Black Market Records."

"Hell yeah, hell yeah… So, let's hear it!"

"I don't know, man, it's—"

"Don't bitch out on me, little homie, we got a long walk. I'll bug you and bug you and bug you and bug and bug…"

Robert giggles again, and then gulps. He hasn't even rapped this one aloud to himself yet.

Heart beating fast with dreadful anxiety, he says, "Ok. But please understand that I only rap in the shower."

"Ok… The shower, huh? So, are we talkin rap or rape?" Kurtis jokes.

Robert laughs pretty hard at that one. What he had written on a random To-Do-List notepad began to marquee across his mind's eye. Trembling between baritone and a pubescent tenor; he raps:

"So tell me why you hate me,
All up in my house just provoking me to go crazy,
All commotion and never shut your mouth
and you tell my momma how to raise me.
I'm boutta just say fuck it,
cuz even optimistically this just persists to be somethin
That I never dreamed of or wanted. And just go off on anyone comin.
Can't stand this shit, can't stand this life I live, and I ain't turnin into you.
Gotta make a move gotta get this fuckin mindstate through
to the world that's burnin you."

While continuing to purposefully step in dog shit, Kurtis yells, "DAMN! Why the hell is this the first time I'm hearing you rap? When I shook your hand when you got here, you should've said: 'Hello, I'm Robert McEvoy, wanna hear me rap?' You've been writing rhymes for a while, haven't you? That's amazing. Kudos to you. I don't ever write anything down. I'm just a fat white boy who's listened to too much Wu-Tang Clan. Ok, I take that back, there's no such THANG as too much Tang!"

"Wow, dude, thanks!" replies Robert. "I've never rapped like that for ANYBODY before! I started writing little rhymes in the fifth grade, they were rock songs at first, and then I started writing rap songs. My heart is pounding out of my chest! Honestly this feels fucking awesome!"

"Fuck yeah brother! I bet it does! I'm not gonna lie, when you said 'Black Market Records' I thought for sure you were gonna rap about eating people. But you didn't, you just held a natural flow like X-Raided. I dig it. Keep that shit up, man, and don't ever give up on writing! Can't believe I just got schooled by a fuckin fourteen-year-old! That's a lot to think about... *DAMN!*"

"Thanks again man, that was fun! You're uuuah! Really uuuah! Good too. I'm sorr... gimme a sec. Uuuah! Uuuah!"

Kurtis's shoes are now coated with dog feces of all breeds. The smell is so terrible that Robert gags and nearly vomits a few times, which is followed by heavy laughter, because even after all that rhyming, he's still higher than bat pussy.

"Holy Fuck! Kurtis! That smell! uuuah! Hahaha!"

Robert of course realizes this is not going to be a friendly visit at the end of this trek. Kurtis had earlier on that month finally explained why he only wears blue. He was jumped a few years back by a pack of cowards all wielding either bats or brass knuckles and hospitalized for almost an entire week.

This particular set of cowards just so happened to be wearing red rags and called themselves the "V-L Eastsiders." Kurtis could only assume he was jumped and nearly beaten to death just for being from the west side, because none of them ever gave any reasons as they stomped and clobbered him.

At that point in Kurtis's life, he was only 13 years old. He was fairly innocent, a scholar in school, and went to church every Sunday with his mom. This unfortunate incident changed him forever. He turned to drug dealing and eventually got loved into a Crip-associated gang known as "Pitchfork." In this gang he obtained street smarts and false loyalty; but quit hanging around them when they wanted to jump in an eight-year-old boy. He'll never forget his roots, though; and despises people who use weapons, bats in particular.

"Remember those dingle-berries I told you about that nearly took my life? I found one of em," says Kurtis as he and Robert come to a stop. "The last one I found got a vile of sulfuric acid shattered on his mug, and, well… This one's gonna stink." Robert stays quiet and nervous, hoping that he won't have to fight anybody. Kurtis calms his nerves by saying "You just stay here, buddy, I'll go handle this myself, and when I'm done, I'll have Paige come get us, so we don't have to walk so far again."

Robert starts to feel better but is also uneasy of the fact that Kurtis's eyes have turned from dark brown to dark black and looks as though he might kill somebody. Kurtis continues, "I'll have Paige roll us a fatty and we'll laugh our happy asses all the way back to the west side! I'll be right back… 5 minutes tops."

Robert stands on the sidewalk and watches Kurtis make his way across the street. One good thing is that it's broad daylight on a Tuesday. Nothing too crazy should happen.

Kurtis walks up to the guy's house and politely knocks on the door. A man answers and steps outside. Robert can barely hear their conversation, but it seems peaceful. All of a sudden Kurtis's voice gets louder, "It's about to be a bad day for—"

"God damn man why do you stink so bad?" interrupts said dingle-berry.

Kurtis then throws a devastating right hook to the man's chin. His whole body flies up two feet off the ground and Robert is pretty sure he saw change fly out of his pockets. Now, collecting dues with dookie shoes, Kurtis proceeds to stomp on the poor guy's face. He stomps a few times, and then finally cleans his shoes off by using the guy's hair as a Welcome-Home mat.

Kurtis makes good on his word. He and Robert get stoned in the back of Paige's Corolla. Paige complains repeatedly about the awful smell and Kurtis responds by saying, "That's the smell of revenge!" They get back home, but their joint is still burning so they hang back in the Corolla. Paige left as soon as the car stopped due to the smell.

"Bobby," says Kurtis out of the blue.

"Bobby?" asks Robert.

"I'm gonna call you Bobby from now on I think," says Kurtis.

Robert never went by Bobby because of his middle name. Robert Joseph McEvoy. If he went by Bobby, chances are people would start calling him BJ. He hated that name. (Especially since Connor and Douglas used to make fun of his initials and call him Blowjob McEvoy.) "Yeah, ok, Bobby's cool. Just don't call me BJ."

"I'll call ya whatever the fuck I wanna call ya. You have no right to tell me what I can and can't say," snaps Kurtis. The mood instantly went from fun and happy to tense and awkward.

"Just go inside and leave me alone. I'll finish this joint by myself," he ended. Robert quietly leaves the car and heads inside. This isn't the first time he's dealt with Kurtis's mood swings. Sometimes it's as though he has multiple personalities. Robert always chalks it up to him being so brutally beaten that there must be significant brain damage. He usually winds up apologizing for these outbursts, but Robert still feels the sting. With shaky nerves he goes into the kitchen and smokes a Red at the table across from Aunt Myrtle.

After a few drags, he realizes he's never asked Aunt Myrtle about the cotton fields. He may not be drunk by any means, but he's plenty high.

"So, Aunt Myrtle, what's the story with the cotton fields, Huh? C'mon ya dirty old bird!" Immediately after those words slipped out, he felt like a little brat that had never been taught manners, or how a boy should speak to his elders, which he had been taught well, but failed miserably with this ignorant start to a conversation. *What the hell is wrong with me? If my father had heard me say that, he would've smacked me hard upside the head!* Luckily, Aunt Myrtle's hearing aids were turned down.

Instead of trying to spark up another smart-ass conversation with her, he stands up and kisses her on the head. She smiles big. All the lines on her face become more visible and her complete absence of teeth makes her bottom lip come up closer to her nose. When he sees her sweet smile, all he can think of is the witch from Looney Tunes that always tried to cook Bugs Bunny; only Aunt Myrtle has no giant pimples and is quite a bit less green.

He sits back down and gets her attention. He motions with his hands pointing at his ears while mouthing the words *"TURN UP."* She understands what he means and turns up her hearing aids. The loud whistle of an old timey radio finally dials in and she signals she's ready to listen.

Just as Robert's getting ready to ask her nicely about her childhood, Kurtis bursts through the door and loudly raps *Nightgown Nipples.*

"Yo! You got them moon-crater dimples huggin nightgown nipples,

Saggin to the floor don't go poppin them pimples!

Cause when Father Time hits you it's so simple and official,

I gots ta get *DOWN* on them Nightgown Nipples!

Peace out Nightgowns! Stay saggin, stay baggin."

Kurtis then leaves the kitchen and heads up to his room, perhaps to conspire with *them* about how and when to destroy the universe. Robert doesn't follow up with any applaud for this rap, not this time. For weeks on end, he has laughed about this song, thinking it was the funniest thing ever, and never realizing until now that Aunt Myrtle's hearing aids may have been turned down every morning. In fact, he's sure of it. The look of sadness and embarrassment on her face is telling him so. She cries into her small, wrinkled palms. Her humorous little old-lady voice is now turning into the saddest thing Robert has ever heard. He tears up, feeling awful, feeling apologetic, and goes to kiss her head again. *SMACK!!!* Kurtis isn't the only one in the house with a devastating right hook, Aunt Myrtle clobbers Robert so hard across the face it leaves a red handprint on his cheek for two hours afterward. *"FUCK YOU! FUCK YOU! YOU COCKSUCKER! YER JUST SHITTIN! YER ALWAYS SHITTIN!"*

Robert had never been yelled at by an old lady before. Her voice was so loud it's a miracle nobody ran to the kitchen to make sure she was okay. But that just seems to be the theme around here: Nobody really gives a shit about Aunt Myrtle. She has no idea that Robert was about to ask her what her real name is and if she had any brothers or sisters. To her, it seems as though he had set her up so she could finally hear those disrespectful lyrics of Kurtis's song. She storms to her bedroom with a painful limp and coughs wildly since the yelling had apparently hurt her throat. She slams her door shut, and now Robert can faintly hear her tiny cries again. For a second there, he was filled with rage after she had rung his bell, completely caught off guard, and then grew confused.

The confusion soon abandoned his brain as she wept in her room. He thought of what it must have looked like to her. Kissing her head, getting her attention, telling her to turn her hearing aids up, and then having Kurtis come in for the big knockout. Seeing situations from all angles was always a gift and a curse for Robert; he would've been better off confused and ignorant. But now, having cracked the case, he feels like a pile of rancid garbage.

He knows it wasn't his fault for her hearing Kurtis's little ditty, he just can't stand the fact that she now thinks he would do something so mean.

But wait, at first I was just gonna pick on her about being a prostitute, so maybe this IS all my fault. I had bad intentions, and got a bad outcome. Shouldn't have I expected this? And all Kurtis did was his usual thing, the usual thing that I've childishly laughed at for almost two months. All the times I've cracked jokes about her, and I don't even know her?! So yeah, I guess I got what I had coming to me. I deserve this red-ass face, and I also deserve to be taken out back and put down like a rabid dog.

When learning valuable lessons, his mind usually punishes itself way harder than it rightfully should. His thoughtful brain is sure to someday slide down his nasal passageway, loogie itself into his throat to be swallowed down his esophagus so it can harden back up and puncture through to the left, stabbing his heart and ending this mental prison once and for all. Needless to say, he had way too much going on upstairs for a fourteen-year-old boy. Speaking of upstairs: he can hear footsteps clunking their way down the two flights. Kurtis appears and pulls a chair away from the kitchen table and sits across from him. His eyes look red and puffy as if he has been crying.

"I can't stop thinkin about that rhyme you spit earlier, dude!" Kurtis says this with smiling puffy eyes as if he hadn't told Robert to pretty much go fuck himself before the whole incident occurred with poor Myrtle. "You're a hell of a kid, Bobby. I think if what your mom is doing with all these men is upsetting you so much, maybe you oughtta just go back to your dad in Iowa." His voice sounds like the usual Kurtis Harper; however, his puffy red eyes and pale skin say something heavy is on his mind. Something much heavier than *THIS* topic.

"Living with my dad is just too boring, and I can't help but feel like Mom needs me around. Just in case one of the men ever tries to hurt her. I don't know what I'd do if—"

"What the fuck happened to your face, Bobby?" Kurtis interrupts as though he hasn't been listening to him at all; his red puffy eyes looking curiously at Robert's cheek.

"Oh, well... Aunt Myrtle smacked me pretty good after you left the room. I don't think she ever heard *Nightgown Nipples* until tonight. I'm pretty sure her hearing aids have been turned down or are out of her head when you sing it."

"Yeah, I make sure she ain't wearing them whenever I rap that one. I'd be a piece-a-shit if I knew she could hear me. She always has them out in the mornings and never puts em in until after her coffee... I'm confused, though. Why did she hear it tonight? Did your little goofy ass sing it to her?" Kurtis open-mouth smiles and chuckles at the thought.

Robert squints and turns his head slightly to examine Kurtis's eyes like a baffled doctor.

"You... You don't remember? You came barging in here and sang it right to her face! Just before you did that, I told her to turn up her hearing aids so I could ask her about who she is and where she came from. Are... Are you fuckin with me, right now? You really don't remember?"

"Wow… No… I can't remember anything after wiping my shoes off on that dingle-berry's head. I must've blacked out again." A minute-long pause falls between them before Kurtis embarks on what Robert believes is that *Much Heavier Topic*.

"I had a terrible dream the night after your encounter with the shadows and the door being slammed and propped shut. I don't even remember falling asleep but suddenly there I was: in my room, sweating bullets in my bed, staring up at a dark black figure. And when I say 'dark black' I mean like my room was already *VERY* dark with no lights on, but this figure stood above me as a clearly visible black hole; like the one you said was in the doorway. I sat up and reached my arm out and when my hand cut through this 'black hole' I felt a charge of horrible feelings; like a bolt of lightning had struck me down and shown me clips of human suffering. Bobby, I shit you not, I've never been so scared in all my life. All I could do was stare at it, or into it, or whatever the fuck you wanna call it. And that's when the black hole spoke with the voice of a sobbing boy *AND* girl; like a child who had just gotten in big trouble and was attempting to apologize.

"I can't remember *EXACTLY* what the fuckin hole was saying except that it was a 'Soul

Reaver', or some shit, that had miraculously escaped the radar of God and Satan. He/she said it had been in Garrisville since the late eighties and when it's done here it'll go state-to-state, country-to-country, until bringing all of humanity to not only a lifeless extinction; but a soulless one as well. After ridding Earth of Heaven and Hell, this 'Soul Reaver' would then be able to birth a new lifeform that would *NOT* be restricted by any form of government; keeping this new civilization free of having to work to live under the almighty dollar. I actually *DO* remember the Reaver saying:

"'The dollar has become far more powerful than both God and Satan. These *people* (it said 'people' with a sick shudder in its voice) of divine creation are a sad waste of life: scrambling like ants under a magnifying glass to get bigger and better material possessions. Satan knows it, and I'm sure by now, God knows it too. There is no place in Heaven or Hell for them anymore. Their souls will be mine now, and so will yours and your loved ones.'

"The Reaver had also assured me that the extinction will be timely, possibly decades leading into centuries. Unless of course he/she can assemble an army to help, and then it asked me if I wanted to join.

"And just then I woke up in what I thought was my own piss but turned out to be my sweat.

I was Drenched. It was morning and the sun was beaming down on me through my window. I felt like I was running a fever. I know it wasn't real because the words of the Reaver were actually thoughts of my own. Not the vanquishing mankind part, of course, but the 'waste of a life' part. Gave me chills.

"Anywho, since that crazy fucking nightmare, I've been having random blackouts. And I deeply apologize if I've been cruel to you in any way. I... I love you, dude. You're the cat's pajamas! And after today I'm convinced you will change the world with your rhymes someday. I just need you to know that my life has knocked me down and put me through Hell, and my mood ain't always the greatest. But that don't mean I don't love ya. Ok, Bobby?"

Robert nods with the response: "Love ya too, man. I think a nightmare like that would make any person go a little crazy. I'm sorry about how shitty things have been for you; makes me feel like I've been taking my whole life for granted. And yeah, I've noticed the anger, but I'm quick to forgive. I mean, I am still running around with my childish mother, ain't I?"

They snicker like schoolgirls, stand up out of their chairs, walk to each other, and hug.

From that point on, the black hole that had been spotted in the attic was never seen again (outside of bad dreams, that is). Noises of male and female moans and cries still haunted the attic as they always had in the past; but no "Soul Reaver," not that either of them believed such a thing could actually be real anyway.

Robert, not belonging to any religion and unsure if he believes there could be a Heaven or a Hell, thought Kurtis's nightmare was absolute bananas.

Kurtis had laughed himself to sleep that night as he thought of how much he had Robert fooled. He was great at making up stories, and this "nightmare" story served as a pathetic excuse for his anger issues. His new little brother was sure to not only trust but respect him now.

(The ugly truth is simply this: Kurtis Harper is suffering from severe schizophrenia, and it was him who had slammed the door shut, wedged the headboard, and climbed out of his bedroom window to watch from outside a shaky Robert tell the other Harpers about a ghost. The noises Robert had heard were tape recordings that Kurtis has obtained from various horror movies. With these tricks combined with the story of a boy named Joey and a girl named Jenny, Kurtis is a regular villain from a Scooby-Doo movie. He keeps people afraid of going up to the attic so he can sit up there "alone" and listen to the new friends inside his mind. And unfortunately, most of these friends aren't friendly whatsoever. They demand blood. There's only one friend that's timid and remorseful, which is why Kurtis had been so inclined to come up with a story and apologize for his random blackouts. He calls this friend Keith, named after his father, and loves this personality dearly. The others kind of terrify him. He knows they're the ones running the show behind his black curtains.)

Chapter 6
Valerie McEvoy

Her mental health is in the crapper, to say the least. These last couple of years have been the worst two years of her life. Her last husband had not only attempted to murder her son, that would've been somehow easier if that were it, but no; apparently if they had stuck around any longer that man might've tried to inappropriately touch Robby. The idea that he may have already done that anyway eats at her even more. Those pictures of little Robby sleeping. Meaning he stood there above her baby in the middle of the night with a polaroid in his hands, or perhaps, just one hand. Valerie tries hard to stop these thoughts, and even as they're fading, Richard Warmurt himself is constantly front and center of her mind. She knows things Robby doesn't know and should perhaps never know.

While Robby was living with William, she had fallen into a drunken downward spiral at her mom and dad's trailer in Stanning. She became a regular barfly at the Pool House in Rosewood and stayed many nights at her ex-boyfriend

Stuart's apartment after closing the bar at 4 in the morning. Stuart was the man she was dating long before she met William. His apartment was conveniently located on the town's square a short walking distance from the Pool House.

Stu-Dog (the nickname given to him by fellow lounge merchants) had tried endlessly to sleep with Valerie and have a serious relationship like way back when and was a nice enough man to take No for an answer. His dopey hope of one day making it happen was the only thing keeping himself available as a drinking buddy. That and the fact Valerie was a beautiful woman. Her hair was platinum blonde (bleach-dyed) at the time with pink streaks down past her shoulders. She was 5'7", not much taller than Robby, with a generous mother's body that earned her MILF-status by Robby's little middle school friends back in Iowa. Her eyes, before recent events, were blue and sparkling. Now, always drunken and swimming with bad memories, her eyes are cold and silver.

She spent an entire six months in this fashion, too drunk for men, too drunk to listen to her parents, and too drunk to care about anything. Until the phone call happened.

She awoke on the couch on a November morning (around the same time Robby and William would be attending a football game in Minnesota) unsure of how she even made it back to her parents' place, still hammered. She peaked out the window and practically hissed at the sunlight but saw that her Firebird was in the driveway. *I DROVE all the way home like this? I could've KILLED somebody! Or myself!* Even in her intoxicated state, this thought was her first sober and unselfish one since April. She stumbled her way into the bathroom and before she could use the toilet, the vanity mirror stopped her dead in her tracks. *I look like shit! what the hell have I been doing?*

After twenty minutes spent crying in the bathroom, she headed to the kitchen and started some coffee. She stood by the counter indifferently; unsure if she should sit at the table and try to read the paper, or go turn the TV on and watch Lifetime on the couch, or perhaps she should just go cry some more under a nice long shower. Yes, the third one, a shower would be nice for multiple reasons.

Just as she was about to make her way back to the bathroom the phone rang. She glanced down at the caller ID and uneasily read aloud what it said: "Cedar Rapids, Iowa. Unknown Number." The thought of how coincidental it was that she just so happened to be at home instead of at Stu-Dog's to be able to take this call that is obviously meant for her never crossed her mind.

She answered with skepticism. "Hello?"

The unknown number from Cedar Rapids turned out to be her friend, Darcy. The friend she was going to call to see if things had blown over enough for her and Robby to come back and restart their lives somehow. *There's no chance of that now,* she had thought. *My little Robby is gone.*

As she fought back tears, Darcy told her that the police had actually never found Richard Warmurt. The suspect they had in custody turned out to be a travelling hobo that happened to be driving the same make and model of Richard's truck. The hobo had stolen it and removed the license plates sometime back in Chicago and had confessed to whatever accusations the police laid upon him so he could get free room and board in jail.

(As they were leaving that awful house on that awful day, Valerie had witnessed a policeman walk into that awful garage. What she didn't know, was just as the policeman entered the garage, he got called back to the station on the news of the hobo. He was ordered to return and continue their original manhunt. Richard had been hiding snug under a pile of old clothes that were to be taken to Goodwill. He had been in there since after he visited the school and ditched the truck in a leaning abandoned barn far outside of town. He had heard his stepson and ex-wife discover his dirty secret, and the phone call Valerie had made to the police. With certainty he was sure this policeman would find him, but was delighted to hear his walkie say: *REPORT BACK TO THE STATION, WE HAVE*

THE WRONG MAN. After the officer left, Richard made his way up to the attic, bagged up all of his valuable possessions, exited the garage, and disappeared.)

Darcy also told Valerie that the local police department had dropped the whole thing as if it were a fluke. Maybe the man spotted holding a rifle hadn't been holding a rifle at all. Maybe the whole thing was a silly little mix-up, stuff like this happens all the time. Never mind the fact Richard Warmurt fell off the face of the Earth, he probably left to start over fresh somewhere far away; most people do that sort of thing after bad divorces. His truck was nowhere to be found. Besides, they had the hobo, and the hobo got his wish fulfilled by getting charged for falsifying information and misleading the police.

Valerie's stomach began twisting and turning like her insides had all been replaced with angry snakes. She told Darcy, "Ok, gotta go now, thanks for the call, I guess," before hanging up and sprinting to the bathroom with uncontrollable diarrhea already trickling down her legs.

After another forty-five minutes of crying and showering in the bathroom; she went back to the kitchen, sat down at the computer desk, and checked her emails on AOL. The majority of her inbox was emails from Darcy. Most of them read along the lines of: *Valerie, I need your number. I have to tell you something about Richard,* and *Valerie CALL ME! My number is…*

She mentally kicked herself in the ass for not checking her emails sooner. Darcy must have found the right number in a phone book somewhere somehow, doesn't matter. This was an all-new series of horrible problems.

Has that bastard been following me ever since? she had wondered. *More than likely,* her mind had answered. *What if he knows where I live? Or God forbid, what if he knows where Robby lives?* She told her mind to shut up, which did not work, but still managed to gather an idea from it anyway. *Indiana. Yes. Her and Robby must leave this hellhole and move to Indiana. 561 miles oughtta be far enough away from that maniac. Even if that fucker isn't actually following us. Can't chance it. Indiana.*

She deleted her inbox and found the friend that told her she was always welcome to come stay with her and her family in Garrisville. She asked the friend if it was still an option and her friend had said indeed it was. There was no need to mention Richard Warmurt. That might actually scare the friend and blow the whole operation to Hell.

There would be no more nights out with Stu-Dog, in fact the thought on its own was a liberating one. She would sober up and find a job and get her son back and leave this mess behind.

It would take some time, sure enough, and it was not going to be easy to get William to let Robby go. But it had to be done.

Now that she's finally here with Robby at a comfortable enough distance away from Richard Warmurt (honestly it felt just as nice to be away from *everybody* back in Iowa), she's slowly slipping back into alcoholism and allowing Robby to do pretty much whatever he wants.

Since she has been in Garrisville she's gone from man to man, not looking for an honest relationship. She had been working as a waitress at an Applebee's when she was offered a job by the manager of the city's rankest strip-joint known as The She Club. She considered the offer for a few days and financially it seemed the right thing to do. She took the job up two weeks later and money had no longer been an issue.

Most of the men she brings home are the toothless patrons of her newfound profession. She kept ahold of her Applebee's shirt and nametag in the back of her Isuzu, so she could change from her stripper attire in a desperate attempt to hide the fact she's a stripper from little Robby, but...

Robert is attending the lowest funded middle school in this ghetto-ridden city. Kids are being hospitalized almost daily for accidentally stepping on other kids' shoes.

His mother never told him she was stripping, and she didn't have to. His fellow classmates were the ones to tell him. Apparently, Valerie had made quite the impression with a lot of the fathers of the students and had even wrecked a few of their homes.

Robert was shoved around and ridiculed every day. "Hey, Fuckface! Your mom gave me a lap dance last night and now I got the fuckin crabs! Same fuckin crabs that got my dad kicked out ya fuckin douche bag!" a bully yelled before spitting toward Robert's face and shoving him to the floor in the hallway. Girls and boys were stopping and laughing at him as he got back up.

Robert was too afraid to fight back or say anything. The last fight he was in, he lost, and that was long before this crazy city where it's known the fights are hardly ever fair with most being five-to-one. Several more weeks went on like that; Robert picking himself up while being hysterically laughed at, and that was much better than the alternative.

With a bit of luck, it all came to an end. A mix between Robert's emotionless reactions, and the school getting wise to who he was living with, stopped the bullying dead in its tracks. He finally started making friends and gained a little respect for how tough he was. But the humiliation still bubbled inside him like a terminal illness.

He absolutely had to get out of that school, and he absolutely had to find a girlfriend so Kurtis would quit teasing him about being a "Queer-mo-sexual."

A few weeks back, Robert and Kurtis were driving around the neighborhood in Paige's Corolla when Kurtis had seen a girl Robert's age walking around the park. "Oh shit, there's Courtney, I hear she's been blowin dudes for money! I got twenty bucks in cash; I can see if we can hook you up lil man!"

Robert's heart began to race. He's only kissed a girl on the lips and that was over a year ago! Kurtis had been hounding Robert that he needed to get laid because he was only twelve when he lost his virginity. And since Robert's now going on fifteen, Kurtis declared that he's got a lot of catching up to do.

Robert with a crackle in his pubescent voice said, "Yeah, sure, I'm down."

They drove up to Courtney and Kurtis rolled his window down. "Hey, I got my little homie here, he's about your age. Can we work somethin out for him?"

"Hand stuff or mouth stuff?" asked Courtney.

"What ya thinkin buddy?" asked Kurtis and he could see standing sweat above Robert's brow.

Robert pulled himself together enough to use his manliest voice and said: "Mouth Stuff."

"You heard the man," said Kurtis. "How much you charge?"

"Well, that depends on how big he is. How big are ya, little man? What are we working with here?" asked a smiling Courtney.

Robert could feel his face turning bright red. He was falling apart inside, practically pissing himself.

"Um, Kurtis. I don't want to do this anymore. Can we please just leave?" whispered Robert.

"Are you fucking kidding me right now?" asked Kurtis and then him and Courtney laughed aloud together in a growing contemptuous sort of way.

Courtney gave a sarcastic little wave goodbye to Robert, pretending her life was ruined having not put his meat in her mouth, and started walking away.

Still laughing, Kurtis rolled his window up and drove back to their house.

"You're such a pussy, dude. I can't believe that just happened. I've never seen something so funny in all my life. I'd be angry with you, but that was honestly just downright sad. Either you have a tiny dick or your just plain queer!" Kurtis laughed and snorted and spat as he put down the person he considers to be his little brother.

Between the kids at school and now Kurtis, Robert couldn't catch a break from being downright embarrassed. He sat quietly and numb in the passenger seat all the way home as

Kurtis took a longer way so he could lay into him with more insults. He was just hoping this was all a bad dream. Of course, he knew that was not the case, so he began to loathe his own existence.

So yes, Robert desperately wants a girlfriend to earn back his *older brother's* respect. He knows the school he's in right now is full of girls who have done nothing but laugh at him. He begs his mom to move schools.

It finally happens; he ends up in a nicer school in a different district. And even though Kurtis calls it the *School for Pussies*, Robert is just happy to not be in a *School for Gang Bangers*. On his first day there he notices another perk: the girls are even hotter in the School for Pussies! His curricular life is starting to look up. His home-life, however, is declining steadily.

Nothing screams *GET ME THE HELL OUT OF HERE!* quite like seeing your own mother walk into the living room at 4:30 in the morning, half-naked in stripper attire, and white-girl-wasted.

"Look at all this money I made, Robby!" yells Valerie. Behind her stands another strange man with his hands all over her. She walks up to Robert, throws 400 dollars in ones and fives into his lap, and runs into her bedroom with *Carlos*.

Robert sits on the couch with all of this money still sitting in his lap and some by his feet.

Stunned and dumbfounded, him and Kurtis have been up all night getting high and drunk themselves.

Kurtis is sitting across the room in his chair just as shocked and asks, "You alright dude?"

This *less-than-beautiful-display* is the first time Valerie has revealed to Robert that she's a stripper. She usually comes home sober and in her casual *waitress outfit*.

Although he had been tortured and bullied for a couple months over his mom's notorious career, reality hits Robert like a ton of bricks. He never does answer Kurtis; he can only remain silent and flushed with humiliation.

Kurtis immediately starts feeling guilty about how hard he's been on Robert. He walks over to him, gives him a big hug, and begins to sob and apologize for everything. Robert hugs back, crying as well. Eventually they break the huddle and start to laugh at each other for how mushy they're being.

"I will never put you down again, buddy. You're dealing with enough as it is. I really hope you understand that I just lost *ALL* respect for your mom, though," says Kurtis.

Robert nods his head, "It's okay man. I don't really like who she's become either. Since we've been here all she's done is whore around and make my life a living Hell." *Just like my father had warned she would,* he thought. He wishes he could call his Dad right now just to see how he's been but thinks it wouldn't be a very pleasant conversation. *This is all,* he thinks, *just fuckin dandy.*

They both get a grip and count the money that's now all over the floor.

"Holy shit there's like *FOUR HUNDRED DOLLARS* here!" shouts Kurtis.

"You know what, man?" he continues. "I wanna make it up to you for how shitty I've been. How bout I take you to that store where we saw that badass sweat suit that you loved."

"Oh yeah," replies Robert. "I almost forgot about that!"

After some much-needed sleep; Robert and Kurtis head for the sweat suit shop. Upon arriving, they see the one Robby's after displayed in the front window.

Kurtis finds a chair to sit in while he waits for Robert to try on the new suit. Robert comes out with a huge smile fitting perfectly into the baggy tan sweat suit. (It came in red or blue as well but they both agreed the color needed to be neutral.) They buy the suit and get it half-price, leaving them with enough money for more weed and booze.

Robert is feeling happy enough to forget about what his mom had done earlier that morning. Kurtis can't get it out of his head. His blood still boils with anger towards Valerie.

Unbeknownst to Robert, it's the boiling blood of a snapping schizophrenic mind; and one of his friends upstairs is sure to be vengeful.

Chapter 7
Robert McEvoy and the Soul Reaver

Oddly enough, the tinkle fairy's nightly visits came to an end shortly after moving in with the Harpers. Robert began wondering what the textbook difference was between night-terrors and bad dreams. His dreams had been undoubtedly bad, especially since the night in the kitchen having emotionally unpredictable table-talk with Kurtis about his bizarre (bogus) nightmare. Just the very thought of the upstairs beyond the doggy-gate in the early hours of daycare, which were impossible not to look upon since they were right outside the one bathroom in this establishment, scared the hell out of Robert to an unexplainable degree. He could feel that blackness buzzing just above him as he made his way for a midmorning whiz, or an afternoon stool, or, heaven save us, an evening shower. He refused to use the bathroom in the treacherous dark from 10P.M. to 5A.M. He'd just as soon hang his willy out the back door and let the breeze take his piss for him.

If there was anything he missed about living in the gravel-dust clouded home off that Dead-End road, it was the freedom to pee outside anywhere and not feel self-conscious. But at least here in Garrisville the smoggy nights allow just enough blindness to his neighbors for him to feel comfortable enough to let it flow.

And here he is, having these bad dreams, semi-consciously pissing outside only after waking from them in a dry bed. Night-terrors seem to keep you trapped until you wet yourself in deep REM sleep while bad dreams wake you up in stupefied horror just in time for a tinkle.

He feels that perhaps as long as there's some sort of older-brother-figure around, the night-terrors will stay away. He had only been wetting the bed while "vacationing"; as he liked to call it because that's just what it felt like; with his parents. It didn't matter which parent he chose to vacay with, as long as his older best-buds weren't around, the Great Lakes were a constant humiliation. The self-respect one loses after waking morning after morning on a soaked mattress is borderline suicidal. Although Robert never saw suicide as a valid solution; supposing he would probably still manage to somehow piss himself in his coffin.

Kurtis Harper may be partly filling a huge void in Robert's life, but he misses his brothers terribly. Even after their last visit had turned sour, it had ended with long hugs and happy tears. He keeps a Wal-Mart Special photograph that had been taken in the coveted Golden Days, framed proudly by himself and facing him on his night-table. A photo of three innocently young brothers with shaggy bowl-cuts, wearing fuzzy ugly-patterned sweaters and corduroy pants, smiling bright for the camera. Condor, Dig-Dug, and Robby in an endless 90's-based adventure behind thin glass. *Welcome to the sweet eternity of Fruitopia and Matchbox Twenty.* He would fall asleep staring into their Golden Day faces. That on its own was more than likely keeping the terrors away, given the fact Robert hates Kurtis as much as he loves him. That love was turning more into a respect out of fear, but it was somehow genuine love, nonetheless. Robert McEvoy has enough room in his heart for everybody, he supposes, except of course for creepy stepfathers.

Up until a couple months ago, as Robert was finishing his remaining eighth grade year in the School for Pussies; Connor and Douglas had done a fine job of keeping in touch with him. They would call once a month and talk for an hour, sometimes two; catching up, shootin'-the-shit, and reassuring their little brother that they would never forget him, that they'd all party down when he came back to Iowa. *Which has to be soon, Mom, right? I think this freakshow's gone on long enough.* But Mom didn't seem to share that idea.

There had been a few times, especially there towards the end, that Robert could've swore on his own life that he could hear something foreign in the background of their phone calls. For example, he kept hearing tid-bits of faint music when the two of them had told him they were using their cordless out on their porch while they smoked cigs and reminisced. Once, Robert had flat-out asked them what they were listening to and they told him they had no such technology for such sorcery, and they all laughed aloud. Robert had chalked this up to being all part of his wild imagination thanks to Sir Dick-warmer and his hamburger phone.

Then the calls had stopped.

(One gloomy day, Christy had accidentally let it slip to Kurtis how high the phone bill had been since the McEvoys moved in. She had meant it in a good-natured, jokingly way and could've honestly cared less since Valerie had been paying half of everything. They were just *ROLLIN'* in that stripper money. Kurtis had then taken it upon himself to buy his own private little phone and hooked it up in his attic to monitor outgoing and incoming long-distance calls. Every time a 712 number would scroll across his caller ID, he would simply pick up his handset and hang it right back on its base. Ending the call permanently because the Harpers did not believe in Answering Machines.

No straight-to-voicemail bullshit, which was all the more convenient. Kurtis had known that Robert would only try to call them around 7:00P.M. because he had listened in on a few conversations and found out that was the Primetime for Connor and Douglas's so-called "busy" schedules. Him and his *friends* upstairs would sit together and continuously do their pick-up hang-up routine every evening from 7:00 to 8:00 as if compelled by some form of maddening hypnotic ritual. All because his mom had joked of a higher phone bill since these little bitches have been around. Robert had drunkenly confided in Kurtis one night and told him he was *DONE* trying to get ahold of those bastards; virtually cutting Kurtis's job in half and making it a hell of a lot easier to play God with the phone lines. Robert had been hearing Kurtis listening to old school rap music just as he could hear Richard Warmurt watching sports in the background of those phone calls. An uninvited third-party line was becoming quite the norm for the young man.)

Despite his new, conflicting views on his older brothers, Robert still sleeps to the Wal-Mart Special on his night-table. But since the phone calls have for whatever reason ended, his dreams have gone from bad to worse. Not wet-the-bed worse, not yet anyway, but sleep was becoming Hell.

His original bad dreams had been in the setting of a dim-lighted gigantic house with a bonus attached garage. This house had touches of familiar features of all the previous (and current) homes he had ever lived in. There had always seemed to be a constant party that consisted of random old friends and forgotten family members (Douglas and Connor never appeared in any of them). They would all be gathered around in the living room, some sitting, some standing, and some fighting. This dream would seem to start off moderately decent in the short duration of catching up with all these old faces. But usually after painstakingly avoiding his drunken uncle from Vespa; ole Uncle Kenney would appear just behind an uneasy little Robby, and say something like: *hey there, Robby —* and that's all Robby would hear before walking fast and nervous like a teenage moron would hobble away from Leatherface. He would then find himself at the other end of the house, far away from his odd company heading toward a bathroom, perhaps to vomit. But as he closes in on the bathroom, he gets coldly distracted by a set of stairs leading up. This stairway was unlike the current and was more like the one from his father's house. Just a set of at least twenty-two dull-wooden steps leading into a barely visible trapdoor. If one were to walk up without seeing this trapdoor, they would certainly crack the top of their head open.

The very existence of the trapdoor gives the atmosphere a barn-like feel, but surely there's more than just haybales and horseshoes up there. He can hear the toiling of a single-handed madman shuffling what sounds like magazine pages while carrying a one-sided conversation more than likely over a phone. Probably that of the hamburger variety. And that's when he realizes he's somehow made it halfway up the stairs. Halfway up the flight of Nope, Not Todays. He begins feeling that all too fresh feeling of falling out of a roller coaster and as he turns around to run back down, the trapdoor opens up wide and slams back shut with a *CRACK!* as loud as Iowan thunder. His legs turn to Jell-O as though to say *Hello! We don't work for the bottom halves of yellow-bellied fellows!*

And he makes a painfully slow escape to the bottom of the... *Wait! Now what's this?* He finds out the barn-like feel is for real and is now standing inside a rundown abandoned horse stable out in the middle of Frognuts, Whogivesafucksville. He is no longer in the giant house attending an awkward family reunion and his sudden loneliness makes him wish ole Uncle Kenney would appear again. Even *his* drunken mumbling would be better than whatever this is supposed to be. With swimming legs, he treads onward and out of the strange asylum and into the clouded night air leaving only a sliver of dim-bulb of the hidden toenail moon as the source of his vision. He can only hope the small shack ahead of him holds his wake-up call, as in this part of the dream he becomes a hundred percent sure he's asleep and trapped inside this dark and misty universe. When he finally fumbles through the fog to turn the knob on this shack, shed, or whatever this is, the door falls from its hinges and onto the paved floor of what appears to be a small shelter of a single, main attraction. A set of homemade ladder steps leading upward into a blinding white light with sounds of children's playful screams and laughter.

And that's when and how he wakes up.

It's also the reason why he immediately checks his shorts and sheets every morning, mystified at how he hadn't wet himself. But these dreams seem worlds worse than the night-terrors. The only justifiable part of this recurring bad dream is the part toward the end: the children screaming and laughing. Simply because as he awoke and regained focus after the dawning shock of dry sheets; he could hear Christy's daycare running at full capacity in the living room, which was just outside the door of his and Valerie's room. The timing of their playfulness synchronizing with the replica of Richard Warmurt's garage-attic-ladder creeps him out by far the most, nevertheless.

The recurrence of these dreams of scary attics and dreaded loneliness was not a tough case to crack. There was the *loveshack* attic back in Northern Iowa, and now there's this new and improved haunted-up-the-fuckin'-wazoo attic right above his very bedroom. And there was also this: *Hadn't he been living in his father's* attic *while melodramatically trapped inside of himself out in the middle of nowhere on a Dead-End Road, feeling horribly alone?*

Why, Yes indeedy-beedy-banana-fanna-fo-feedy!

The worse-than-bad dreams began invading his rest shortly after not receiving his anticipated monthly phone call. His childish, insecure feelings of no longer being loved by his older brothers seemed to conjure up a real shitshow. Deep down he knew they weren't the true cause. For these new dreams starred a fresh cast.

They started off seeming like the original (the *O.G* of bad dreams, if you will), inside the gigantic house with the usual mature- and child-aged awkwardness as per usual. Only the role of ole drunken Uncle Kenney had been replaced by an unfamiliar woman who seemed more like a foamy-mouthed ghost that insisted on going to the other end of the house. There was something terribly wrong going on upstairs, she would tell him. She would then begin to shout *THE SOUL REAVER IS REAL,* but her voice never seemed to raise a decibel. It almost sounded as though she were screaming under water, or from a thick-glassed prison cell. She persuaded little Robby toward the staircase by telling him she needed a strong man to push the trapdoor open, for it would be far too heavy, as if something were sitting on the other side. As they reach the bottom of the steps, the foamy-mouthed ghost transforms into a striking young woman approximately Robby's age.

He could never remember, no matter how hard he'd try, what exactly the girl in this new dream looked like. All he could dig up was there had been an instant chemistry and her eyes were wild with love. For all he knew, this girl was his soulmate. She was, after all, the girl of his dreams. He would very soon come to think otherwise. Words between them were never spoken, they could only stare into each other's eyes while they made their way up the stairs like a bride and groom up an altar. They would only break eye contact when nearing the top and Robby would valiantly shove the trapdoor open. He would then find himself alone again, thinking his new girlfriend must've said "Nope, not today!" And so he stood there alone in the cut-out square with the trapdoor resting atop his noggin to see Kurtis Harper having a *friendly* chat with a seven-foot tall black-buzzing apparition. He felt his body suddenly float closer and closer like a camera zooming in to a dramatic scene of what appeared to be a one-sided conversation. The black hole didn't speak, it only buzzed like a swarm of horseflies snacking on a dead Wildebeest. Somewhere in that buzzing was a rap song almost positively produced by Death Row Records. Scared out of his wit and nearing a nervous shit, he looks back toward the trapdoor in hopes his girlfriend came back. Hell, he didn't care if Jennifer the Foamy Ghost came back. But what he sees instead is his mother. She's standing in the cut-out square just as he had been with the trapdoor resting atop her head. But she's crying. Weeping would actually be a better way to put it. Until this dream, he had never seen dear Mom in such agony, and he's seen her cry plenty of times. This cry seemed to suggest a last goodbye, *either I'm gonna die or your gonna die so let's just say bye,* kind of cry. As he tries to move his legs and finds out they've become Jell-O yet again, his mother gets yanked away and out of sight causing the trapdoor to slam shut. It was as if she had been pulled hastily down the stairs by some crouching boogeyman. His mother's screams fill his ears and then fade away as she's carried off to perhaps one of Connor's or Douglas's nightmares. He stares into the empty void of where she used to be, more terrified than ever. His father's voice blares down from above as if this crazy attic had been lined with PA speakers with his dull monotone voice behind a microphone:

YOU CAN'T JUST LEAVE HER LIKE THAT.

Holy Sperm-Whaled Fuck-bubbles, Batman! I gotta wake up!

His mind drifts away to when he spent the summer with his dad at the Mechanic Bootcamp. The radio in the shop always played the *moldy-oldies,* as William liked to call Classic Rock.

The song by The Animals, *We Gotta Get Out Of This Place,* begins to grow slightly coherent through the very PA speakers Dad was just speaking through. Eric Burdon's vocals suddenly degenerate into what sounds like a sad demon and all the instruments are now warped and out of tune. It sounds as if it's on vinyl spinning in slow-motion atop the world's oldest turntable.

"If It's The Last Thing We Ever Do." Perhaps from the record player of Satan.

As distracting as the music is trying to be, Robby can't help but feel like he's being watched and suddenly thinks it might be a good idea to look back toward Kurtis and the giant swarm of blackness. The look on Kurtis's face as he stares at scared little Robby holds odd resemblance to that of Sir Dick-warmer's murderously perverted stare. In fact, he's no longer sure who the man is sitting across from the black hole. It's some kind of twisted figure of all the men he's ever seen his mom with. And here he is, floating uncontrollably again, the camera closing in for a major climax, Robby is sure of it. The closer he gets, the faster the faces change on the strange couch-sitting man. He gets right up close and personal to the now blurry lump of silly putty on the couch when his mother's agonizing screams yell for him to run and the lump quickly becomes Kurtis again. He and Robby are toe-to-toe, and the Harper who a second ago was an inanimate figure of talking wax stands with a discombobulating suddenness, grabs Robby by his shirt collar, and pulls him in so they become face-to-face all in the matter of two seconds. Kurtis's eyes grow black as the thing that is now behind Robby. Shark's eyes. And as he shoves little Robby into his good friend, Mr. Soul Reaver, he mocks the weeping of Valerie *(Run, Robby, Run!)* with a revolting, yellow-toothed smile.

That's when Robert wakes from this new breed of dream, falling out of the roller coaster, into the Soul Reaver, and onto his bed. There had been no children's playful screams or laughter at the end of this thrill-ride because this particular dream was somehow quite shorter, and Robert would awake in the pitch black of four in the morning; making it all the more scarier and harder to cope with. It seemed to take an eternity for his night vision to kick on and he was sure that when it did, he would see a giant black shadow hovering just above him.

When it would appear the coast was clear, he'd leave the room and take a long, rewarding, half-awake piss out of the back door.

He wasn't so sure he could go on living as a sane person if this particular bad dream started to revisit him like the prior one had. His mom and dad being in this one made it way too personal. And why was this woman starting off as a bile-spewing ghost turning first into his girlfriend and then into his mother? *Hey man, what the fuck, Joe?*

He had suspected he would dream of the "Soul Reaver" at some point since Kurtis had embedded it into his brain. But it seemed to him that Kurtis himself was the main antagonist of the dream. Why would that be the case? Did he really fear Kurtis that much? What was he saying to the Soul Reaver? Why did it look like he was planning something with it? *THE SOUL REAVER IS REAL! No, not by a long shot, tuts, but I'll tell you what IS real: Kurtis Fucking Harper. How could this dream not be some kind of warning? If it isn't, I'm losing my goddam mind.* These thoughts would swirl sometimes into midday more than once a week, because despite his pleas to never dream like this again, these bad and worse-than-bad dreams would alternate nights like two parents fighting over custody.

I must just be projecting my own bad history onto Kurtis; Robert would conclude on days after the worse-than-bads. He really did love Kurtis. The guy could be hard to handle even in small doses and was great at belittling his supposed "little brother" but for the most part Robert knew he meant well. And seriously, the guy's been through a *LOT* of rough-n-tough shit. Yep, scared little Robby could awake from those warning signs and still justify his love and respect (fear) for Kurtis. He was unaware of all the Scooby-Doo tricks and was even more unaware of his secret little phone. Sure, it was no hamburger, but it had the power to tear Robert and his brothers apart, and that's what it was exclusively used for. *There you go, Bobby! Who's your fuckin Brother now?*

Eventually the bad and worse-than-bad dreams became his *only* dreams. On opposing nights, he'd sleep in nothingness, a powered off TV offering no form of bad nor good. No offering of a needed variety. Just two bad, bad, very bad dreams. It was also becoming more and more difficult to justify his feelings for Kurtis, whose attitude was worsening by the minute. Robert was more than ready to depart the Bipolar Express. His mother, again, had not yet shared these feelings.

He finally decided that these nightmares really were warning signs, but what was he supposed to do? Every time he'd try to ask a question or deviate from the dreams' original outlines, he'd teleport to where he was needed and be forced to stick with the script. These dreams started producing more problems than the self-esteem lowering bed-wetting he was so glad to be rid of.

The Wal-Mart Special on his night table began to seem to laugh at him and provide zero Golden Day comfort. It absolutely had to be thrown across the room and broken out of its frame in a childish tantrum and his mommy had to be the one to put it up in the attic because scared little Robby didn't want to be eaten by a fucking SOUL REAVER.

Perhaps these dreams have put me over the rainbow, toys in the attic.

Say, I love attics, don't I Joe?

Sure do, Bob.

Hey Joe, could I bum a smoke from you by chance?

Sure thing, Bob. Feel free to fall asleep with that still smokin, Bob, so maybe we can burn to death in bed before we wind up French-kissing our girlfriend/mother in our new dream and wind up coma-toast.

Hey man, what the fuck Joe?

Yep, much like Kurtis, little Robby is gaining some friends in his attic as well. But Joe and Bob don't seem to have a mean bone in their make-believe bodies, no sir, nothing like Kurtis's friends. Rest assured, he's still got a handle on things. He hasn't soaked a mattress in over a year, so how bad could his mental state really be? His father would most definitely be proud of him now, maybe even proud enough to take the ungrateful little fucker back someday.

Chapter 8

It wasn't long after he got the news of his son and ex-wife's departure to Indiana that William McEvoy had ridded the world of Richard Warmurt; a pedophilic waste of a human, whom, could very easily be forgotten.

The weeks following the dreadful court date had been the most trying of his life, and he was sure life would remain meaningless and empty until Robert awoke from his crazed dream and returned home. *What is my boy doing right this very moment?* He would wonder, then fill his dead-end-road-homestead with screams of depressed agony. The screams made him feel like a lunatic, but were they actually *screams* if no one else was around to hear them? How could he allow that monster of an ex-wife to take his son on such an irresponsible escapade? More importantly, how could the *State of Iowa* allow it? The situation had grown beyond his control and that was something he had never prepared for. Having his way had always been a ceaseless ease of his life, until now. So, he'd scream by day and cry by night until falling fast asleep on the floor of the room his son had occupied during the time that had become *his* Golden Days.

The memories that were made in that short timespan have become a double-edged sword of sweet serenity and bitter tears. The better the memory, the sharper the stab to his heart. All day long he would torture himself by holding conversations with his imaginary-but-real son.

A lot of songs remind me of the good old days. You know, Dad, the Golden Days? I hear them and can smell what I used to smell at our old house and get goosebumps. The good kind of goosebumps.

Son… YOU *are the Golden Days. And I'd give anything to hug you right now and tell you how sorry I am for making you feel so alone.*

That's when Oceans of Fun began to roll down William's face. The thought of himself walking away from his son after he had reached out for a hug on that last day they saw each other; really makes him wish it had gone differently. That he would've immediately embraced the boy with a father's support and whispered to him: *I love you no matter what you decide and will always be here for you if you change your mind,* which very well could have altered the current situation drastically. He would feel more comfortable calling his son more often, or perhaps his son would've changed his mind right then and there and would still be here today. This not being the reality, he goes to the empty two-roomed attic and hugs his son's pillow while reciting what needed to be said. What the boy needed to hear from his father on their last limited time together. The pillow still withheld Robert's scent and even provided temporary comfort, but it never did hug him back.

He had done a bang-up job guilt-tripping Robert and is now working overtime without pay, guilt-tripping himself. There were so many things he could've done differently. So much more they could have discussed. And he couldn't get it through his thick skull that Robert was just a child and no matter how hard William tried, or how differently he could've done things, the boy would've still wanted to live with his mom. Valerie held a sort of hypnosis over Robert. It had been that way since he was a newborn. William had admired it tremendously when their family was whole and despised it with a rotten green jealousy after the divorce.

The Big D. *This all stems from you and me, Val. There's no one else to blame but ourselves. The two older boys will never speak to us again and our youngest will ping-pong between us in an unfair endless match of "I'm the better parent. No, I'm the better parent," until he's old enough to emancipate himself and never speak to us again either.* The art of separation shows no discrimination, for it devours and divides all parties involved.

His pride had allowed him to continue working at his uncle's mechanic shop. They had warned him long ago that something like this would happen. Little snotnose Robby would run back to his mommy and leave Big Bad Bill all alone in his remotely located mansion. How right his uncles had been, and how wrong he desperately wanted to prove them later on in life was the only motivation for getting up at the crack-ass of dawn and dealing with the two old pecker-heads.

Although the shop was equipped with pneumatic impacts and hoists; William insisted on using good old-fashioned wrenches and car jacks. Using his muscle was a tremendous release of frustration, and his uncles couldn't see him crying underneath a vehicle atop a slab of cardboard. He refused to let them see how hurt he was, both mentally and physically. There had been a few times that one of them had to kick his legs to make sure he was still alive because he had fallen asleep under a car with depression-induced exhaustion. It didn't take but a couple weeks for them to notice their nephew's pity party and so they fired and replaced him with no signs of remorse.

The firing hadn't been such a bad thing. The long drives to and from the shop were becoming hellishly quiet. Too quiet, save his uncontrollable thoughts. He never dared listen to the radio; that would only bring more double-edged memories. His son had been sitting in the now empty passenger seat sharing his dreams of becoming a musician while they listened to that radio. And if Collective Soul's *The World I Know* should happen to play, he was sure to smash apart the face of his factory-included AM/FM/Cassette player with contradicting emotions. He never realized listening to his own thoughts was much worse for him, nor would he have cared if anyone had told him so. He was not to listen to any form of music until his son returned home. He would then buy his son a guitar and listen to whatever amateur melody would spew from its amplifier. Then he might be able to listen to the radio again.

The travels to the shop were never as equally terrible as the travels from the shop to his empty home on the Dead-End road. Robert had jokingly told him that the place sometimes reminded him of Alcatraz, to which William snarled and said there was plenty to do on their rented land. But now Alcatraz seems to be appropriately fitting. At least without those long and lonesome travels home he can just remain put in his own prison without being spoon-fed the harsh reality of how far away it truly is from everything else. He would have to move away soon, this he was sure of; because every time he heard or seen a vehicle nearing his dead-end island, he would be filled with hopes of it being Valerie returning the precious cargo that is his son, only to be disappointed as it trailed gravel dust further and further away from his house upon the hill.

The court-date had been February 26, 2002.

It was June 5th of the same year when he first noticed Richard Warmurt driving slowly up and down the hill of the dead-end road. Of course, he hadn't known for sure who it was until he finally decided to set the sights of the scope that was mounted atop his Colt AR10 rifle and magnify the obvious face of the puke who haunted his son's dreams.

Like Robert, William wasn't aware of the nasty items in his garage attic. However, he was well aware of the psychological and physical abuse this man had bestowed upon his son. And how this man made his son quiver as he told him about how he thought Dick-warmer (that nickname made William laugh aloud) had some sort of sick sexual obsession with him. The very fact this man had found where Robert had once been living and was stalking the area was proof enough that he meant to harm his son. But obviously Dick-warmer was ignorant to Robert's current whereabouts, which was just peachy, considering the crosshairs zeroed in on his neck at the present moment.

William McEvoy was an excellent marksman. In his hunting days he had put bullets between the eyes of many deer with uncanny symmetrical precision. He took pride in finding the sweet spot within his high-dollar Leupold scope on his bolt-action Savage .308 rifle. That rifle was his baby long before his first-born son, Connor, was around. He put his hunting behind him shortly after Douglas was born because his alcoholism was growing into borderline woman-beater; and hunting and boozing went hand in hand. He quickly sobered up and sold the Savage. It had turned into a constant reminder of the piece-of-shit he had never set out to be but was almost becoming, and the gun seemed to beg him to drink and shoot. This again spoke much of William McEvoy's character. He was a man of many mistakes but was also quick to turn his life around before being overrun by his inner demons. Unbeknownst to his family, he had purchased the Colt AR10 back in '93 with no intention of falling into his old habits. He had only used it for target practice and found he was just as gnat's ass accurate with the Nikon scope as he had been with the Leupold on the shooting ranges of various locations. It had become a healthy form of release, and though he hadn't shot it in almost a full year, he would not be rusty.

He had only originally grabbed the Colt to use as a form of telescope, because he hadn't owned binoculars since the boozing days. He had seen that the car, which was clearly a silver Pontiac

Sunfire, had been parked in an almost cocky fashion in broad daylight at the bottom of his driveway, approximately 75 yards from where William is now. As he slightly cracked the window to prop the muzzle of the gun on its sill, he could hear no evidence of the car running. For it was in park and turned off. He zoomed in first on the face, which appeared to be looking upward as his neck was fully extended, the man looked as though he were in deep thought and staring at the ceiling of his Sunfire. It was obvious to William that this was in fact Richard Warmurt because he had seen an ugly picture of his undeniably scarred face that was taken from his and Valerie's wedding. His head appeared to be completely shaven, as well as his face, as if he were trying to hide his hideous identity. This feeble attempt of disguise made no fool of Big Bad Bill. *How convenient it is*, William thought, *that this gun just so happens to be fully loaded with Winchester 168 grain Law Enforcement hollow points. Also,* he deliciously continues, *how convenient it is that his car just so happens to be parked on a dead-end road in the middle of nowhere.* He then maniacally says aloud as if Richard can hear him, "Welcome to Alcatraz! You belong to the island, now!"

With the safety still on, he pretend-fires three bullets into Dick-warmer's neck. Marking each fake trigger pull with a whispered *"BANG."* *Am I really going to do this? CAN I do this?*

His trigger finger works the safety off as though to say, *Yes, you can, and yes you will.*

He cocks the gun without losing focus and for-real fires three bullets into Richard Warmurt's neck, killing him instantly. The windshield of the Sunfire explodes and blood sprays from the driver's seat as if his body had been replaced with a giant red spray-paint can that squirts, then stops, squirts, then stops, repeat. William's vision from the scope only allows a nasty mess of red, and so, dissatisfied by his view, he props the gun against his couch and ventures out of his house and down his driveway to get a closer look at his prized game.

On his way down the lane, he starts to feel immediate regret. *What the hell am I thinking? How am I supposed to live the rest of my life with this blood on my hands? I'm going to have to turn myself in. That's the only step in the right direction from here. I might even get a reduced sentence if I tell the judge 'I was in fear for my life'.* His thoughts race this way and that as he approaches the vehicle.

His close-up view of the interior of the Sunfire changes his mind instantly.

The creep had obviously been masturbating. Whether or not the faggot-ass-stepdad had finished, William could care less, nor would there be any way to see pre-existing fluids amongst the re-painted interior of the silver Sunfire, and to his maniacal satisfaction, red is a good look. What is not a good look was this slack-jawed yard-ape with a stifled dork clasped in its paw.

William, in a fit of disgusted anger, begins rapidly punching the fucker's head that is now dangling from its shredded neck. He punches until the head flies clean off, breaking away from the remaining tendons and flesh. It ricochets from the passenger door, and lands on the floormat at the foot of the passenger's seat with a wet thud. William shakes with blind rage, only seeing the blood coated all over his trembling fists, and screams.

He isn't sure how long he had been mumbling nonsense on his front lawn, but it seemed to be growing dark, and luckily for him there had been zero gravel travelers this afternoon/evening. He forces himself to take care of his new problem. Turning himself in is no longer an option. This freak of nature, or whatever it is, does not deserve the sanity and freedom of William McEvoy. The scene of the crime can no longer be deemed as an act of self-defense. This fucking thing deserves to be burned from history as a never-was. Nobody should ever be subjected to learn of this strange event. Burned from history, burned from existence, and most hopefully: burned from memory.

This now very conveniently located dead-end-road-homestead has yet another perfect feature that almost makes the whole thing feel premeditated. For the landlord, who never seems to care what William is up to and has never dropped by to check on things, had dug out a giant burn-pile pit for the fallen trees and limbs that never stand a chance for Iowa's harsh winters and springs. It's a 15-foot deep by 20-foot long and wide hole made for the sole purpose of incinerating Mother Nature's mistakes. Richard Warmurt and his silver Pontiac Sunfire not only fit the profile, they would also fit comfortably at the bottom of this blackened earth which was now fresh and ready with winter and spring's disasters long since burned. Yes, this hole was ready for this summer's disaster, which just so happened to be this dead troglodyte that is William McEvoy's first and only murder victim. And he'd be Goddamned if the idea of a strong drink didn't have him stricken with cottonmouth; after all, he did just get done hunting.

Looking into the car as least as possible, he covered the corpse in an old black comforter that he had never been too fond of. He then opened the door and shoved the covered carcass to the passenger seat to be with its head. The car started without hesitation, just as William had suspected it would, since this whole thing seemed meant to be, and he drove the Sunfire toward the pit with Richard Warmurt's headless body sitting neck-first on the passenger seat with his legs hanging halfway into the back of the car.

William grins madly at his companion and says aloud, "Buckle up, Fuck-O! Next stop is Hell!"

He got the car into the pit by pulling up close, putting the Sunfire in neutral, and pushed with such force the car had flipped on its nose and landed on its back. William had retreated to his house to grab from atop his dust-covered China hutch a 17-year-old 1.75L glass bottle of Wild Turkey that he had kept unopened as a sign of strength. Then to the kitchen for an old hand towel and a box of matches.

He had half the bottle gone by the time he reached the pit and was feeling swimmingly well. He told the overturned Sunfire to go fuck itself and then laughed at the idea of the headless cadaver's hand still possibly clinging on to its wiener. Then laughed even harder at the nickname his son had given this animal.

"Dick-warmer!!! Ha Ha!!! You're about to be 'A-Lot-warmer' you *SAVAGE JACKASS!*"

He pulls another few swigs until the bottle is quarter-way-full and shoves the hand-towel down its neck. He takes twenty steps backwards while attempting to light a match; somehow managing not to fall on his ass and catching his own self on fire.

The third match gets the job done and without having to try very hard, he tosses the flaming bottle into the air and watches it make its way down into the pit. From his distance all he can see for a while is a thin smoke-line until the car explodes into hellish fire.

William McEvoy is far too thirsty to stick around and roast some mallows nor can he play a choppy version of Kumbaya, My Lord on an acoustic guitar. A short intermission to the liquor store for more whiskey is the only logical way to man this fire. He may need more wood to keep it aflame and knows of a fallen tree just north of the fire pit half-on and half-off of his property. He had left it there to see if anyone else would claim it and save him more work, but now this work is mandatory, and let's be honest, downright fun. There's nothing quite like catching a buzz on a lawn chair in front of high flames under an Iowan cotton candy sunset.

He'll keep the fire going until the skeletal frame of the Sunfire is the only thing left. Then he will dispose of said frame at the salvage yard located near his uncles' shop. In small-town Iowa nobody makes conversation or thinks twice when they see a charred-up car frame. Burning demo cars and old beaters is a common hobby.

And that's how William McEvoy conveniently and successfully made Richard Warmurt disappear into thin air. It's also how he fell back into love with his old friend, liquor.

There would be no moving from this Dead-End road now. He owns this house upon the hill just as much as he owns the life and death of Dick-warmer, the sticky-handed ghost.

Chapter 9
Harvey and Andy

Margaret Coffman sat patiently in her chair waiting for her husband, Harvey, to return home. He had left almost an hour ago for groceries, claiming, "Tonight's going to be extra special, Margey, just you wait and see." And although she didn't hear a lick of what he said, she waited.

The two of them have grown old together, *too old* if you were to ask either of them, and tonight Harvey wants to surprise her with a home-cooked meal to celebrate their 40th wedding anniversary. Harvey, a man who has only been known to make no more than a grilled cheese sandwich or Kraft macaroni and cheese with hotdogs, had watched enough reruns of *Cookin' Cheap* to work up the nerve to attempt something out of his comfort zone.

At the store in the meat section, Harvey stands leaning over the meat counter with his head tilted up while his eyes dance side to side looking downward through his small spectacles at the end of his nose; licking his lips and mumbling like the old man he's become. At one point he scratched at his butt and farted loudly and held back hysterical laughter in exchange for a small chuckle with watering eyes. Being old was a funny thing to him, and he laughed more at himself than anything else.

On his seventieth birthday he decided he was old enough to play practical jokes on people in public, the likes of which would be embarrassing to any man younger than 50. He began dressing in the usual geriatric fabrics that never seem to change through time as if for a thousand years these same clothes have been marketed for grey-tufted-old-fogies. He'd tuck his button-down shirt into his pants and hike his trousers up past his belly button, leaving almost a foot of space between the bottom of his powder-blue dress pants and his black moccasins, revealing his long-checkered socks. He liked to pretend he was just an ignorant old fool and walk around every day with his fly undone and his tucked-in-shirt hanging out of it a few inches. He would walk about proudly with his elbows out and his crotch front and center while his feet pointed outward. It was a hilarious sight to see him, at a humbling 5'7"; walking from place to place with a shit-eating grin and a tilted fisherman's cap atop his head. People on the streets are hardly ever aware of his undone fly with the shirt sticking through because his smile has always been a contagious one. But if you were to ask anyone from the west end of Garrisville, they would tell you his choice of outfit was a real knee-slapper. He is dressed this way now, in the store as he farts and chuckles.

He doesn't even need the spectacles; it is also part of the act; both his eyesight and hearing are fully functional, but he enjoys yelling *HUH?* All the time and when his eyes are squinted to make it seem as though he can't see, it's all the easier to disguise his constant devious smile. The only thing that seems to be deteriorating other than his body, is his memory.

"Okay, let's see… I got the fresh garlic, the red potatoes, the green onions. Ope! And let's not forget this asparagus, yes, the asparagus. God forbid we forget the asparagus. Now, do we want chicken or steak? Let's see, we ate steak at that one diner for our last anniversary, so's I guess we'll go with chicken. Yes, chicken."

The man behind the meat counter was also the owner of the grocery store. His name would be asked for, then answered, and again forgotten by Harvey. He was having a tough time recently with names. Harvey didn't care much about that right now anyway. All he really wanted was 18 ounces of chicken. "Will that be all, Harvey?" the man behind the counter asked.

"Yes, I do believe so, young man. Thank you."

Scotty Fossberger was the name of the meatman/store owner, and he found it very sad that Harvey couldn't remember his name anymore. In fact, every employee of the store began to feel sorry for Harvey. It was obvious he was suffering from Alzheimer's. That's what their statements from the Hoosier Newspaper read back in the spring of '97, anyway.

With his chicken, garlic, tators, green'ins, and asparagus; Harvey makes his way to the check-out lane where Tony the cashier stands smirking as always behind his register. Harvey likes Tony a great deal. Mainly because he knows the young man is wise to his forever-polyester-boner hanging out of his trousers. Which is why the boy is always holding back laughter behind a smirk. He thinks Tony may be the only one (other than his wife, of course) who knows his old man act, is indeed, just an act. But he has to take the glasses off the end of his nose to read the young man's name tag every time he sees him lately. Damned if he could ever remember the funny boy's name.

"Hey, uh…Tony!"

"How's it going, Mr. Coffman?"

Another reason he appreciates Tony: Tony is always Respectful. A trait that seems an endangered quality these days. Harvey Coffman would tell anybody who'd ask the right questions that Respect will be fully extinct by 2010; give or take six years.

"Pretty good, can't complain. Came in to get a few things. Tonight's a big night for me and Margey! It's our 40th! Can you believe that? My gosh! And I still love that woman as much as when I first met her!"

"Congratulations, sir. Oh, and how's she doing after the operation, anyhow?"

"Well, let's just say she really loves her chair at the moment, but that'll change in good time. I know we ain't no Spring Chickens anymore but Mrs. Coffman's a hell of a fighter."

Respectful cashier Tony began to almost feel worried. Harvey's expression suddenly went blank and dull as if he might suffer a stroke right this very minute.

But finally, his eyes glimmer and a bigger grin than the one he's usually wearing touches his face in a full-on smile. Tony was then astounded at this man's love for his wife.

He was actually daydreaming *of her. Right here in the check-out lane!*

"Your total's going to be seven dollars and twenty-two cents."

"Here's a ten. Keep the change, uh… Tony. Don't wanna keep her waiting much longer."

"Why, thank you kind sir! Happy Anniversary, Mr. Coffman! Oh and…"

And that's all Tony could get out before the door was shut behind Harvey on his anxious endeavor. Again; Tony was awed by the amount of love that could still be alive after a whopping *forty years* of marriage but was also sad that Harvey had forgotten his bag of asparagus.

Harvey made it home in record time. He was pacing at the equivalent of a fast-walking youngster when he got into his house and made immediately for the kitchen. While un-bagging his groceries, he yelled aloud to his wife who was still sitting on her favorite chair in the living room:

"Hey, hun! Just got back from the store, gonna whip us up some grub!

No, not hot dogs and mac n' cheese! I'm talkin about *REAL* food!

I didn't buy any onions, for chrissake! *Not white ones, anyway.*

You just mind your own and watch the tube, woman!

Okay, sorry… I know it ain't the 50's no more!

Love you too, hun!"

An hour and twenty minutes later, Mr. Harvey Coffman was ready to serve Mrs. Margaret Coffman her fine and surprisingly decent-looking meal. Harvey had really outdone himself. He placed the two made-up dishes of baked chicken and garlic red potatoes (with green onions), onto a clear-orange party tray they had gotten as a wedding gift ages ago; and also placed two glasses of Merlot on either side of the tray. He then untucked his shirt and zipped his fly; for this was no time for fooling around; and brought the party tray to the living room, paying no mind to the forgotten asparagus.

"I love you so much, my Margaret," he said with tears in his eyes as he kissed Margaret on the forehead and handed her a plate of his masterpiece of culinary art.

He brought his own chair up closer to hers and changed the station on the TV from *Seinfeld* to *Married… with Children*. For a seventy-five-year-old man in the year of 1996, he was hip to all the current television shows. Most people his age (not including his wife, of course) despised the new-aged television shows.

Anything after MASH *is garbage!*

Margaret always had a funny saying: *If you can watch* The Fresh Prince of Bel-Air *without laughing; get the fuck off my porch!*

Mr. and Mrs. Coffman were rare breeds, to say the least.

"Ope, yep… You Caught me!

Green onions taste different than white ones!

Well, if you hate em so much, don't eat em, woman!

Okay, sorry… I know it ain't the 50's no more!

Love you too, hun!"

As Al Bundy notoriously shoved his hand down his pants; Harvey thought it well to light some candles and dim the lights. *The more romance, the better!*

Of course, the burning of the candles may have only been used to mask the awful smell that's become overwhelming in this last month, and he may have dimmed the lights in a feeble attempt to hide the sight of the rats eating away at his wife's feet.

Mr. and Mrs. Coffman's 40th anniversary took place in June of 1996. It wasn't until after Tupac Shakur's death in the fall that two middle school aged boys discovered the rotten corpse of Margaret Coffman on their walk home from school.

"*PETER TAP!*" yells one of the two boys as the other boy falls to his knees after receiving a less-than-gentle tap to the nuts.

"Man, what the fuck?" exclaims the peter-tapped victim holding his groin and red in the face. "That's not cool, man, and you know it."

And Kurtis Harper's best friend at that time, Jeremy Knight, did know well enough hitting another boy's junk wasn't cool; but it sure was funny!

"Oh, come on, Kurty! Don't be such a *PUSSY!*"

"Stop callin me Kurty, asshole! And I probably wouldn't be such a pussy had I not gotten so much of it from your mom last night!"

"I'll stop calling you Kurty when you stop calling me Jerry, Fuck-Wad! And keep my momma's pussy out of your mouth."

"Sorry, Jerry, but my mouth is the only place your momma's pussy knows anymore."

And with that all being said, Jeremy picked up a loose rock from the side of the street and chucked it hard at Kurtis with the careless consideration of a pre-teen. The rock hit Kurtis squarely on his hairline and goose-egged almost immediately. The Rockwar had begun!

They ran to the lot of the Sunny Bread factory's semi-trailers where the entire ground was loose gravel rock; three blocks away from the factory itself, straight across the street from the Coffman residence. After approximately twenty minutes of flying rocks and hard-to-explain bruises; they called truce to their weekly match of Rockwar and huffed and puffed away from the Sunny Bread trailer yard with bloodied teeth and bumpy heads.

Jeremy and Kurtis held each other up as they crossed the street, so beat out of their minds they wound up on someone's front lawn; didn't matter whose; they were high on their own adrenaline and Kurtis found the perfect moment for perfect payback.

"PETER TAP!" Kurtis screamed as he didn't just *TAP* this poor boy's peter; he *PUNCHED* it.

Jeremy Knight dropped to the grass and cried harder than ever; he didn't even scream this loud after falling on his tailbone from off the top of a trailer during one of their Rockwars.

Damn it, I punched too hard again. Jerry ain't gonna want to hang out for a while now, thanks to this.

But before the two of them could debate their future friendship; Jerry caught a disturbing glimpse through the window of the house whose lawn they were now on, on his way back up for air. And when Jeremy Knight pulled a double-take and saw that what he thought was a terrible hallucination was actually for real; his mind snapped.

His first thought was:

Norman Bates's basement. Leatherface's bathtub.

His second:

My EYES can smell her.

Third:

Through the smoggy windowpane sat a smiling skeleton; dead for centuries; gathering moss.

Forth and foremost:

What's black and white and red all over?

This nightmarish gelatinous sculpture before me, that's what. Never knew a corpse to void its bowels more than once yet here it sits in MONTHS worth of its own shit.

The rats had long moved from her feet and were now feasting upon her face. They had grown fat with human flesh, and one appeared to be the size of a small dog.

Her eyeballs had been eaten away; the blood which had been drained from her sockets was now a dark purple. Black is actually the color the boys had testified within this grotesque discovery. What was left of her face were two large empty holes, a half-eaten nose, and a wide-open mouth with rat tails coiling out of it. Jeremy Knight screamed aloud in terror, sprinted home, and told his parents about the Coffman house. The parents called the cops and when two policemen and an ambulance driver finally arrived, Kurtis Harper was found staring through the window at what was left of Mrs. Coffman. Officers Grindle and Schultz suspected the boy was traumatized by what he was seeing and frozen with fear. When in reality, Kurtis was in deep thought of his recently broken home.

Kurtis Harper, having seen what drove his best friend insane, could only think of his father and how he had left a few weeks ago. He stared through Margaret Coffman's corpse and thought of his father's decaying love for his own two children: him and Tabitha. He hadn't taken the time to let what happened actually sink in until now, in his newfound alone time. And while he was deeply hurt by his father's departure, he couldn't imagine how badly Tabitha must be feeling. It was one thing for his father to leave them behind, but another to witness his little sister's heart break as she read the note he had left for his family.

Dear Christy and kids,

I have found the very thing I have been searching for all these years. Happiness.

While Kurtis and Tabitha grow older by the day and fall more out of love with me for who I am, a flamboyant man seeking companionship, I grow colder and hold a resentment toward them, for which I cannot explain, other than the fact they were born from false love.

The man I've met has not two, but three children who have all been enlightened by the lifestyle I crave and show no signs of harsh judgment.

I warned you time and time again that church was not my place and yet you took the kids anyway for them to become Fag-haters.

Christy and kids, please know this is not your fault. This WHOLE THING was a huge mistake.

Just know that I am finally happy and feel that I belong to a TRUE family.

     XOXO
     -Keith Harper ☺

Whilst Kurtis thought of the note from his father, Harvey Coffman watched his beloved Margaret get lifted onto a stretcher in a body bag. This was the first official realization of his wife's death, which according to the paramedics, occurred four months ago after a failed surgical removal of a brain tumor. The newspapers will eventually say that Harvey Coffman suffered from severe Alzheimer's disease, which wasn't untrue, but in reality, he just simply never let his wife die, in his mind. True love can be as funny as a polyester boner every now and then. His love for Margaret did not die with Margaret; nor did his fantasies of having her around. When his beloved Margey started complaining about constant headaches and fear of death; Harvey started to hold conversations with her in his mind and acted as if none of it were true.

It can't be real! If I'm not dying, she CAN'T be dying!

Luckily for Harvey, the District Attorney had seen no foul play within the evidence provided and sentenced him to two years in Garrisville's finest mental health facility: Wormwood Springs, which the good people of all-ends Garrisville would tell you is the hellish equivalent of Arkham Asylum. Only Batman will *NOT* be there to save anyone.

Officers Grindle and Schultz each paid a visit to the two young boys' homes a month after the unfortunate incident. Grindle visited with the Knight family and Jeremy seemed to be handling everything quite well. He told Grindle the only bad thing that came out of the whole deal was that him and Kurtis no longer spoke to each other.

When officer Eric Schultz made his way up the front porch to the Harper home; Christy Harper greeted him kindly and invited him in. They sat at the kitchen table after Ms. Harper persuaded an old gal she called Aunt Myrtle to leave the room. The kitchen stunk of burnt coffee and cigarette smoke. Ole Aunt Myrtle had apparently been hot-boxin' it up all morning. Christy asked the officer if he wanted anything, and he declined respectfully by saying he had a heavy lunch when in truth the stinky kitchen made him lose his appetite altogether.

"Not even coffee?" Christy asked.

"No thanks," replied Schultz; trying like hell not to vomit on this nice woman's floor. "If you don't mind, I'm just gonna come right out and ask. How's the boy doing?"

"He's okay, I guess. He's napping up in his room right now, I can go get him if you—"

"That won't be necessary, ma'am. Let him rest. I'm sure he needs it after what happened last week, poor little fella."

"Have you guys found them hoodlums who almost killed my boy?"

"No, ma'am. Afraid not. Detective Golden is still on the case... Ms. Harper, I hate to say it; but in a city like this with a crime rate that nearly matches Gary, chances are we'll never find them. Your son refused to give us any sort of description of them, and according to Golden, the boy seemed to be lying about not remembering what they looked like. Now I'm not saying that I believe your boy is a liar or anything like that; personally, I'm not very fond of that prick, Golden. But the only lead we have is that they were all wearing red. There are seven different gangs in this city that fly red flags under the Bloods; seven that we're at least aware of, anyway. That doesn't give—"

"Alright, that's enough!" Christy suddenly snapped and began to weep. "If you're not here to update me on any suspects then *WHAT THE FUCK IS THIS VISIT ALL ABOUT? ARE YOU JUST DROPPING BY TO REMIND ME? I DON'T NEED REMINDED! IN THE SPAN OF JUST TWO FUCKING MONTHS, MY POOR SON HAS HAD HIS DADDY LEAVE, DISCOVERED THE SAD OLD MAN'S DEAD WIFE, AND THEN WAS SAVAGELY JUMPED BY A PACK OF FUCKING—"*

"Please calm down, Ms. Harper. I really didn't mean to flap my gums about how the case is going, or about that goddamned asshole, Golden. I have no say whatsoever on how that case is to be handled or anything, for that matter. I'm just a pee-on who happened to be on-call the day of the incident with the Coffman house. Officer Grindle is visiting with the Knight family as we speak, we both thought it well to see how the two young men are doing. Seeing a thing like that... I can't even imagine... I've overstepped my boundaries by coming here today, such lousy timing. I'm very sorry, ma'am. I'll be on—"

"Christy. You can stop this ma'am crap and call me Christy, please. I ain't as ancient as turtle Myrtle in the other room! I should be the one apologizing, Mister..."

"Welp, if I'm to call you Christy, I guess you can call me Eric."

"Alright then, Eric. You sure you don't want any coffee? Myrtle makes it nice and strong."

After the roller coaster of emotion that just passed between the two of them, officer Schultz was ready for black coffee *AND* a pack of smokes. "Yes, please and thank you."

After three cups of Aunt Myrtle's famous joe; Eric Schultz sat rambling on like a madman at the kitchen table with Christy and Myrtle (she snuck back in at some point) about how him and officer Grindle were long-time friends and joined the force together, even graduated from the same academy and everything. He told them how their first call had been horrifically more than either of them bargained for and how they would be scarred for life. But they get through it all, one day at a time, and have counseling sessions (separately, they ain't married. Not yet anyway, Ha-ha) weekly to help ease their traumatized minds.

Long-story-short: By the time Grindle and Schultz were called upon for the Coffman house, they were veterans of PTSD. They knew, however, that the two young boys who witnessed that nightmare were nowhere near as mentally prepared. That's when they mutually took it upon themselves to check in on them. They felt that it all had happened for a reason (because policemen are *NOT* allowed to believe in coincidences, Ha-ha). Christy was growing tired of his stupid little jokes and if he laughed aloud one more time in this house; she was going to 1-8-7 on this motherfucking cop, Ha-ha! But all jokes aside, she understood why the two cops felt the way they did. Kurtis's good friend Jeremy is black, and officer Grindle is black as well. It isn't the rarest thing to see blacks and whites befriend in Garrisville nowadays but back in '96 it was practically unheard of. Unless of course you belonged to a gang, where the only color that matters is the clothing you wear, you were more likely to see an elf with a unicorn than two friends of opposite colors.

When Schultz was finally done talking about himself; he realized he hadn't learned anything new of how Kurtis was handling all of these… developments. "Back to why I came here in the first place, how is the boy?"

"Well, he has taken the devil's wrath and other than sleeping a lot, he's handling everything much better than I would've ever expected. The only thing that I can actually tell is getting to him, is his father walking out on us. It just doesn't make sense that he left the way he did. He sat me and Kurtis down last year and told us about his… well, his sexuality. I told him that I respected him for telling us the truth and Kurtis told him he'd always love him no matter what. Tabitha was never supposed to learn of any of this, at least not until she was much older. We were gonna work through it. I was gonna let him have his extra-curricular activities on his own time and we would remain together for the sake of our children.

"Shortly before he up and left us, Keith began to grow paranoid that we all hated him for who he was and was hanging out with a 'friend' who was known to be a crack-addict. He left us with an awful letter that I had hidden away from the children and somehow Tabitha found it. She took the letter to Kurtis and they read it together, so I'm told. At that time Kurtis seemed completely fine; then the Coffman house; and then the 'jumping' or whatever the hell these thugs call it. And on top of all that's happened to Kurtis; Tabitha hasn't been eating well since her father left and she's starting to look scrawny and sick.

"In my heart I feel that we just need to leave this terrible place and start over fresh somewhere, but my maiden name is Prey, and any Preys of my relation are long dead. I have *ZERO* family in the U.S. that I'm aware of. This house's rent is dirt-cheap, and the landlord is very lenient on when he gets paid. I've grown to love my daycare kids and it all just seems hopeless to leave. We, like everyone else in this God-forsaken city, are stuck here."

Whilst Christy pours her heart out to Officer Eric Schultz, Harvey Coffman sits in the Rec Center of his new home, Wormwood Springs. He's been crying uncontrollably at random since he laid eyes on his wife's body bag. Cries himself to sleep, cries himself awake, doesn't cry for an hour or so, and then cries when he sees something as simple as a napkin. *EVERYTHING* reminds him of her. Or at least reminds him of the *idea* of her; because now that her body has officially been taken away and out of sight, his Alzheimer's is making him forget what she looked like. Soon it will be worse, and that's another reason he can't stop crying; he's going to forget her altogether. He mourns for not only the loss of his wife, but also the loss of the memories they had made together over 40 years.

Seeing her every day, rotten corpse or not, reminded him of the kind of man he is/was. Reminded him of the tucked-in shirt, spectacles, fisherman's hat, and hiked-up dress pants with polyester boner gag every morning. Now that she's gone, he's forgotten all about his silly ways. Now that she's gone, he really is an ignorant old man. He knows he was once the happiest man on Earth until the body bag came along, and that is all.

He begins to see his new home as a hospice for his mind, he soon won't remember a thing about himself or his wife and will therefore be as good as dead. Especially if Nurse Becca keeps trying to feed him what she likes to call "Happy Little Pills."

Wormwood Springs' reputation was only reviewed poorly due to most of the occupants who were court-ordered to stay there. It was the home for kids who murdered their parents; women who killed their husbands in "self-defense"; grown men/women who were caught diddling little kids; arsonists, school-shooters, and old men like Harvey who were slowly losing their minds.

The good citizens of Garrisville were soon to find out that the people who went into Wormwood Springs voluntarily were just as, if not more dangerous than those who were sentenced.

A man by the name of Andrew Wallabee Pfister had checked himself into Wormwood back in 1990 for more reasons than one. He had been bullied all through elementary and middle school for his unfortunate name until a nice boy named Joey stood up for him. He grew to become best friends with Joey from that day on until he got drunk and accidentally dipped his willy into Joey's girlfriend, Jenny. Just when he was about to shoot himself like his good friend, Joey; his dad came in and slapped the rifle as it fired. No real damage was done, other than permanent hearing loss in Andy's left ear, and Mr. Andrew Pfister The First decided it might be a good idea to tell *NO ONE* of this incident. Andy had only heard half of what his father had said and checked himself into his local psych ward the following day. He's currently (1996 currently) banging an ugly nurse named Becca Beckins who feeds him "Happy Little Pills" that keep him horny and dangerously insane.

When Andy heard the news of the old creep known as Harvey Coffman, he knew he'd get to meet the man very soon and was looking forward to it. Him and Nurse Becca had been doing some terrible things to the elderly men of Wormwood for the past two years.

Becca Beckins had confided in Andy in the spring of '94 that her father had been sexually abusive her whole life and how she couldn't help but be absolutely disgusted by men older than 50. Andy suggested she try a dose of her own medicine; that maybe all she needed to think clearly was her own "Happy Little Pill."

She took his advice, smacking herself in the head for not thinking of this genius plan sooner, and has been ingesting the pills with Andy ever since, growing hornier and crazier as the days progress.

The "Happy Little Pill" she had been giving to Harvey was actually a knockout medicine that was commonly used for date rape, which was not the same as what her and Andy had been popping but what they used on the unfortunate old men that disgusted her greatly.

Their first victim had been accidental. But their greed for more caused the second, third, fourth, fifth, and sixth. Wormwood had been far too overpopulated and understaffed for people to notice these disappearances, and Harvey Coffman was going to be their oldest victim yet.

They were a couple of crazed pill addicts; anxiously waiting for their opportunity to teach Harvey a harsh lesson on how he shouldn't have become an old man and upset poor Nurse Becca like he was doing.

Andy and Becca had found a hidden crawl space that led into what appeared to be an old speak-easy from the prohibition era. Its dirt floor is home to six shallow graves, soon to be seven. It is also where the two of them have nasty sex and sometimes step on uncovered corpse noses. The putrescent smell has become a noxious gas that further progresses their crazed intoxication.

Harvey Coffman had been suspicious of Andrew and Nurse Becca since his arrival. They hadn't done that great of a job keeping their relationship secret. That and they both seem high out of their minds. So, when Nurse Becca would offer him a "Happy Little Pill," he would put it in the corner of his mouth and gulp down the paper cup of water without ingesting whatever terrible medicine it must've been. He would then thank her for the medicine, go back to his room, and spit it into the toilet. He would notice anxious shadows of footfalls outside of his door an hour after pretending to take his pill. He would do things like turn his TV up louder and cough or use the john and flush the toilet to make whoever was outside his door know he was awake and aware of their presence. Then he would hear angry voices and see the shadowy footfalls disappear. *We're dealing with some very odd people, Margey,* Harvey thought. *We gotta get out of this place.* And then with the famous Animals song in mind he sang aloud, "If it's the last thing we ever do."

Chapter 10
Connor and Douglas

Douglas Avery McEvoy (aka: Dig-Dug or Duggy) loves his brothers more than anything in the world. He currently lives with his older brother, Connor, and they are both working at the same job as roofers with a shabby crew outside of Cornbelt, Iowa. Connor simply didn't seem to care when they were suddenly unable to reach their little brother in Garrisville. Duggy, however, couldn't stand it. He and Robby had become best buds before their parents split up and can't help but feel that his little brother is in some kind of trouble. Luckily, Valerie had let them know the address they were staying at in case the boys ever wanted to write or send something for Robby's birthday.

And for Robby's fifteenth birthday coming up in August of 2003; Dig-Dug decided he wanted to make a mixtape of various rap songs he had illegally downloaded from Morpheus. He had no way of knowing that his little brother was currently not listening to *ANY* music due to his horrible nightmares or the fact that his depression had pushed him further away from his dreams of being a musician. Over several weeks of adding, deleting, and re-adding songs; Douglas made not one, but two burnt CDs for his little brother. It was only June, though; so he was going to wait and send them at the end of July in hopes they'd make it in time. With a fat-tipped Sharpie, he wrote in his coolest form of handwriting on both CDs: **Happy Birthday Bro! 2003 Mix!** And then placed them into an envelope with a sappy letter he almost found embarrassing. He grew overwhelmingly excited for his little brother to hear some Paul Wall and Chamillionaire and was having a hard time not sending the CDs early.

Finally, on the morning of Friday, July 25th; he decided he had waited long enough and dropped the envelope into a blue box with postage affixed to his little brother's unfortunate residence in Garrisville.

Connor and Douglas had graduated high school; Connor in 1996, Douglas in 1999, and were planning on working instead of going to college. They would do some roofing in the summer, and work at their local Pamida in the winter. Connor forced himself and Douglas to set aside a generous sum of money from each paycheck so when they actually decide on what type of degree they want; they can afford it a little easier.

When it came to older brothers; Connor McEvoy was by far the best. He watched out for Douglas constantly and kept the clumsy shithead out of trouble. It wasn't that he didn't care about not talking to Robert anymore (he was just as upset as Duggy), he simply felt he had to remain strong and tell himself they would all be together again soon. He understood that Robby and Duggy had become very close because the same thing had been happening between himself and Douglas since they left their parents' house. And no matter how big of a shithead Duggy could be (getting into fights with hicks at bars, or falling asleep on railroad tracks), Connor would always be there to help him fight or wake him up before being run over by a train. Even though they were only three years apart, he almost had a sort of fatherly love for Douglas. But an incident a few weeks ago had really tried his patience. Duggy almost got his ass handed to him by Connor himself. This particular incident had also changed the course of their lives in a permanent fashion.

It happened on July 4, 2003. Connor will never forget the date not only because it's a holiday but because he has the police report and will keep it around forever to remind Duggy not to be such an airhead. He was awakened at 4:30 in the morning (meaning the dumbass was out partying the night *before* the fourth) by a phone call from the police saying that his brother was trying to break in to Pamida so he could steal some flip-flops.

"We haven't taken him to jail yet," said officer Bartlett. "We are still outside of Pamida with Douglas in the backseat. He's very drunk. He's bawling his eyes out and begging us not to take him in. If you'd like to come get him, we'll let him go. You boys haven't been much trouble, at least not until now, that is."

Connor sat at the end of his bed in his underwear, thinking: *Goddammit, Duggy! What the fuck, man? No officer, we haven't been much trouble because* I'm *always there to save his ass.* He almost told the officer to take him to jail so he could just go back to sleep but instead said this:

"Would it be too much to ask if you take him to jail and I come pick him up from there?"

"No, um, I guess not. May I ask why?" asked officer Bartlett.

"He needs to learn something from this. He needs to know I'm not always gonna be readily available to drop everything and bail him out."

"You're an excellent older brother."

"Could you do one more thing?"

"Yeah, what is it?"

"Make sure you make him think he *REALLY IS* going to jail. Put him in the cell and everything. Preferably solitaire. But when we hang up, I want you to tell him I ain't coming to get him and I'll take my sweet time to get there. Is that okay, or have I asked for too much?"

"Nope, that's just fine and dandy. Thank you for your time. I'll let Douglas know you ain't comin to get him." Officer Bartlett hung up and smiled.

By the time Connor made it to pick up Douglas, officer Bartlett had really played everything out as asked for, and then some.

"I typed up a police report and told him he has a court date next month… All bullshit! And he believed every word of it, too! Here, you can keep the report!"

"Thanks officer, that's awesome! Hopefully this'll teach him not to be so damn childish! Where's he at?"

The fact that his brother had gotten caught by the police and that he was called in the middle of the night/morning to come save him *AGAIN*; wasn't really what pissed him off the most. It was their conversation on the way back home.

"Where the fuck are your shoes?"

"I muth have loth them thomewhere between Tapperth and Pamida, ahuh!" Douglas McEvoy had developed a speech impediment in the second grade which was corrected by years of speech therapy but nowadays he talks like Daffy Duck when he's drunk. "Thath why I wath trying to get thome flip-flopth. Then all of a thudden I wath tackled to the ground! They were beating the back of my legth and I farted in their faceth, ahuh!"

"Why would you be at Tapper's when you know we're supposed to work tomorrow?"

"Becauth roofin really thuckth a bag of dickth."

"Sound out your fucking S's, Duggy! You're spitting all over me!"

"Th— Sorry. I juth—just didn't wanna work tomorrow. I felt like drinkin instead. Who gives a flyin shit anyway! As long as Robby's not—"

"Stop fuckin talking about Robby. I'm sick of it. Every time you get drunk you blubber on about him. There's nothing we can do about it. He's a fucking Momma's boy!"

"Okay, yeah, fair enough. But he ain't near as much of a momma's boy as you were a fuckin Daddy's boy when you were his age! He's still our brother! You just don't even seem to give a shit about him anymore!"

Connor had then made Douglas walk the rest of the way home.

Barefoot.

Lately Connor can't help but feel that Duggy was right. In his heart he knows he's always loved Robert, but they're a full decade apart in age; it's hard to sympathize with someone so much younger. It's easier just to call him Momma's boy.

On July 25th, the same day Douglas mailed out Robby's birthday gift; Connor sat down with Duggy and told him they would go to Garrisville in August to surprise Robby for his birthday and see if maybe he'd like to come back to Iowa with them.

"Are you serious, man? Like furrealzy's?" asked Duggy.

"Yep, fuckin-A radio, brochacho!" replied Connor.

"What about my court date?" Duggy's eyes grew big and concerned.

"What *about* your court date?" Connor responded with laughter and Duggy followed suit.

The trampoline trio would be together again.

Friday, August 8th, 2003 had started like any other Friday with the two of them driving to work together, listening to *Pussy Crook,* by Mystikal, in Connor's 1988 Cutlass Supreme. Connor insisted on listening to that song *EVERY* morning, claiming it got him pumped up and ready for work. Douglas had a 75 disk-holding binder full of burnt CDs. Ten of which all had *Pussy Crook* as track one, and then a variety of other songs afterward. These CDs were all labeled **Work Mix!** And he couldn't wait for Connor to no longer show interest in that song. This particular work mix had been scratched up badly enough it could only play *Pussy Crook* and force itself to eject on the second track. Duggy was grateful for this. He had heard all ten work mixes at least 15,964 times. When he made Robby his Happy Birthday Mix, he burnt an extra two copies for himself. He un-sleeved the first disk of his latest 2-disk mixtape and popped it into Connor's CD player.

They had both recently installed two new subwoofers into the Cutlass and the bass they produced rumbled deep enough to literally take your breath away. If you were to sit in the backseat; you would first think you were getting the massage of a lifetime, and then would grow concerned your eyeballs could just shake loose from your skull. So, when Twista's *Adrenaline Rush* began vibrating throughout the car, both Connor and Duggy got as pumped up as the song was referring to. Duggy had been in love with the entire Chicago/Rap-A-Lot Records scene since Do or Die came out with their album "Picture This" and changed his world with *Money Flow*. The latter was actually track one on Disk 2 of Robby's Birthday Mix. Rap-A-Lot Records was always about representing the Midwest, and Duggy ate that shit right up. And now recently, a Texas Invasion had been blowing away the rap industries; catching even the ears of young midwestern white boys. Big names like Slim Thug; Bun B and Pimp C; Mr. Pookie and Mr. Lucci; Z-Ro The Crooked and Trae The Truth; Paul Wall and Chamillionaire; were becoming huge all across the United States with a fresh take on love for money backed with an old-school-style composition. Distinguishing themselves with ease away from the typical club shit. Dig-Dug's double-disked Happy Birthday Mix was by far the greatest compilation of Shot-Town and Houston. It held a natural flow. It seemed to symbolize the world as one to Duggy and when he listened to this mix, he not only thought of Robby, but of humanity itself. It was, in its own way, highly educational; and he couldn't wait to pass all of this knowledge on to Robby.

Connor had apparently felt the same way, even though he hadn't been following any rap-related propaganda since the death of his favorite rapper: 2Pac and would never be able to tell Mr. Pookie & Mr. Lucci from Do Or Die. Connor was very much into it, to say the least, and grew even fonder when Duggy told him it was the same mix he had sent to Robby for his birthday.

They were halfway to work when Connor stopped at a gas station for a 30 pack of Stones and decided him and Douglas were to play hooky and do some daydrinking. These two awesome CDs needed their immediate attention. They were leaving next Thursday for Garrisville anyway and had saved enough money to not care about their job. This is no longer a typical day in the neighborhood for Connor and Duggy; this is *Gravel-Travel!*

Song after song, beer after beer, road after road; Douglas reached into the case and noticed they were getting low on beverage. They were on the outskirts of Grisly when Connor made for the Casey's General Store located just outside of town. He went in with a sober-enough-looking composure and bought four shooters of Jack Daniels with a One Liter of Coca-Cola for a chaser, and an additional 30 pack of Stones, just to be safe. He had to be sure they wouldn't need to stop again.

It was only 2:00 in the afternoon.

All of the McEvoys share an additional trait to bad nerves: they can all drink like fish. Their alcohol tolerance is much higher than the average human. Therefore, while other people would be sloshed and passing out behind the wheel at the point that Connor and Duggy have both reached; they are in fact just getting started. That doesn't mean they can't get wasted. It just takes a while longer is all.

By five o'clock it was safe to say they were wasted. But here again, unlike most people, Connor and Duggy can maintain a wasted state for a decent amount of time. Connor made a decision he probably should have made three hours ago and stopped the car. They parked outside of Tim's Tavern in Stanning. A hole-in-the-wall bar that isn't very easy to find because it has no signs. Not even a neon *OPEN* sign. What it does have is a pool table, a jukebox, and a bartender who will serve any drunkard any amount of liquor; even if said drunkard is pissing himself on his barstool.

Duggy was beginning his speech impediment and told Connor to:

"Go get uth thome quarterth tho we can play thome pool and lithen to the jukeboxth!"

"Damn it, Duggy! You're spittin all over me again! And stop yelling!"

"*THORRY!*"

"Ok Dig-Dug the Daffiest Duck we know, what shall I get your majesty while I make change, O Holy One?"

"Rum and Dr. Pepper."

"There you go! Keep saying words without S's, Brochacho, and save me from your spit!"

"Go fuck yourthelf, Condor!"

"Don't threaten me with a good time, Broham Dilly!"

Connor made his way to the barkeep just as Duggy began to hump the pool table and rub its green felt as if he were groping at breasts. These are usually the kind of things that get Duggy into fights. People just can't accept him for the weird, goofy stunts he pulls. Connor loves his younger brother even more for these reasons but is highly relieved nobody else is in the bar at the current moment to witness what Duggy is doing. Connor orders their drinks and leans on the bar looking back at his goofball of a brother; proud as a peacock and laughing because it may just be the funniest thing he's seen in a long time.

He gets their drinks and $10.00 in change and heads back to the pool table that Duggy seems to be satisfied with and is smoking a Camel on a chair next to it.

"Gimme thome quarterth! I'm gonna go play uth a few thongth!"

"You're yelling again. You didn't say please. And it's my turn to pick some music. You've been music Nazi all day with your Mr. Dookies and your Military Lizards. And I'm ready for some *ROCK-N-ROLL!*" Connor gives Duggy a preview of his Awesome Air-Guitar skills and Duggy could only smile and shake his head. They were practically from different worlds, but neither of them would rather be anywhere else than where they are right now; with each other as always.

"Oh, thank God! I thought you were gonna try to find Puthy Crook, ahuh!"

"I highly doubt that juke-box has *ANY* rap, just look at where we are dude! Stanning's—"

"Are ya gonna go pick a thong or are ya juth gonna thtand there and thuck dickth all night?"

"Am I offending your girlfriend?" Connor nods toward the pool table.

Duggy rubs the table's slot mechanism for the quarters and says:

"She'th juth ready for uth to play with her ith all. Here, thmell my fingerth!"

"Hard pass, brochacho! Think I'll just leave you two alone for a while."

They got a solid five games of Nine-Ball in and made it entirely through Alice in Chains' *Jar of Flies* before a group of familiar faces walked into the bar. Connor and Duggy had somewhat sobered up; playing pool slowed them down a bit. The effect of drinking all day long still hung above their heads like buzzing halos, though.

They were surprisingly quite excited to see some of these faces. It was a few people from the class just below Duggy. Apparently, some ladies and gents from Cornbelt's Class of 2000 had been pretty much doing the same thing Connor and Duggy had been doing all day. Of course, in moderation. For they weren't nearly as banged up as the two McEvoys. *What are the odds of us seeing* these guys *all the way out here in Stanning?* Connor thought. *We're lucky we didn't collide into each other on our way here.* And that's when he realized how peculiar it was for him and Duggy to be here in Stanning, in general. They hadn't meant to visit their old town, but there they were.

Connor later found out the Class of 2000 was stopping in Stanning for a pre-game warmup before questing on to a house-party somewhere between their current location and Rosewood. There was said to be plenty of coke for anyone willing to come out. Connor and Duggy's eyes simultaneously lit up, they hadn't done any blow since 9/11! They asked around if they could tag along and the Class of 2000 said yes, indeed they could.

More than anything, Connor was excited for them both to sober up a bit. The buzzing halo above his head was heavy and he knew with certainty his younger brother's halo was even heavier. (It is common knowledge that if you are drunk as a skunk and happen to fall down and accidentally snort a line of cocaine; you will no longer be drunk, but uncontrollably social, and any beer afterward is only felt the next day.) "Count us in!" yells Connor. The bartender had overheard everything and wished them all good luck, caring only about how great his business had been.

About a half an hour later they were simultaneously disappointed. They had ridden uncomfortably in the far back of a 2001 Suburban for an endless amount of time while the "youngsters" listened to the new Shinedown song on repeat all the way to some country house where the coke was promised, but entirely sniffed up. There was still plenty of booze left, though, and plenty of people willing to hang out and talk.

The excitement of the cokeless house-party made them both run outside and vomit. It was a three-story house, and it was full top to bottom with "youngsters" yakking like a misplaced truck shipment of defective Furbys. Also, to put the icing on the cake, the new Shinedown song was playing inside the house on surround sound. Connor absolutely loved the new Shinedown song until it was played for a third time in the Suburban and apparently picked up where it left off in this house. It was beginning to feel like The Twilight Zone.

After puking some of what they had been working for all day, they decided to go back in to drink more and educate these kids like Cornbelt High never could.

It didn't take long to get right back to where they were, and Connor saw Duggy sitting next to some kid on a couch, yelling in his ear and spitting on his face about the "Texthath Invasion."

Then Duggy wrapped his arm around the wet-faced victim and said:

"I love you, Robby."

The kid on the couch leaped from where he sat to puking on a plant in the corner.

Connor had been busy talking about baseball with a random fifty-five-year-old man who claimed his friends call him Zander. But that didn't stop him from hearing what Duggy had said.

Connor immediately felt sad for him. He was even planning on going over to some hot young chick after talking to his new friend, Zander; but decided to plop on the couch next to his brother instead. The dread of not having their own vehicle to be able to escape this place hit him like a ton of bricks.

"You doin alright, Duggy?"

"Yeah, I'm good. Like *REALLY* good! A guy upthtairth had a little bit of blow on him."

Connor's sadness changed to anger upon hearing this news.

"*WHAT?* You did some fucking blow without me? Where's this fuckin guy at?"

"He'th probably thtill upthtairth, calm down, dude!"

"Well, wow, now that you fucking mention it, how bout we go the fuck *UPTHTAIRTH?*"

Duggy always hated it when Connor made fun of his speech impediment, and Connor knew it. The sadness that was replaced by anger now came back to Connor full force.

"I'm sorry, buddy. I didn't mean to make fun of you. I—"

"Ith all good, Robby! Ith juth nithe to have you back!"

Apparently Duggy has just enough booze and blow in his system to think *EVERYBODY* is his little brother, Robby. Connor grows worried but is far too anxious to go upstairs to say otherwise. "Take me to your Master," is what he later regrets saying.

They make their way toward the staircase with Duggy falling down repeatedly and Connor picking him back up. When Connor was finally done practically carrying Duggy up to the second floor; Duggy said: "Nexth floor, Robby. He wath on the third—"

Duggy began to fall asleep in Connor's arms. Connor shook him awake and that's when Douglas McEvoy appeared to catch his second wind. Or his third, or fourth. Connor wasn't sure. But he had to run after Duggy like they were playing a game of *TAG* up the second flight of stairs.

On the third floor sat a circle of more "youngsters" hiding away from the rest of the party, passing around a small glass tray and a rolled-up twenty-dollar bill.

This is it! Thinks Connor. *This is where the REAL party is!*

A few people sitting cross-legged on the floor huffed and puffed about these two Fuckheads barging in, but the person who seemed to be the one running the show offered Connor a line.

"Dude, your brother was just up here! He's fucking hilarious! It's an honor to meet you, Robby!"

Holy Shit! Connor thinks. *How long has Duggy been running around here talking about Robby?* Not wanting to seem like he wasn't in fact Duggy's brother, Connor says:

"He's a riot! Always keeping me on my toes, that's for sure."

"Man, I gotta pith!" says Duggy, obviously having to pee.

The man apparently running the show cut a more than generous line for Robby, or Connor.

"Just open that door and go piss, good buddy," says the guy running the show.

The glass tray was then passed along to Robby/Connor and Connor/Robby was more than grateful for this huge line of distraction. Connor then says aloud:

"This is for you, Connor!" and just as he's sniffing up his generous portion of coke; he's unable to see Duggy open a door, walk through it and disappear.

Everybody sitting on the floor immediately starts shuffling and trying to figure out how to deal with what they just witnessed.

Connor ignorantly takes in his entire line and says, "Thank you, Robby!"

He was alone now, hearing a bunch of clunking down the stairs and people shouting frantically, unmindful of the sudden draft in the air from the door Duggy had opened. And, of course, he could hear *45* by Shinedown playing on the first level for the hundredth time. It wasn't until after helping himself to a few more tootskies that he went downstairs and saw the entire house was empty. It was The Twilight Zone all over again.

He walked around the outside of the house yelling for somebody, anybody to answer. It was three o-clock in the morning now and the sky had reached its maximum darkness with a touch of wet fog you could almost choke on. Connor walked slowly with his arms out front of him, beginning to feel his stomach turning and demanding a nervous dump.

And two minutes later he tripped over his dead brother.

Douglas Avery McEvoy (aka: Dig-Dug or Duggy) died of a freak accident on the morning of August 9th, while simply trying to use a bathroom that wasn't there. He fell out of a door that led straight to nothing but the hard ground below, breaking his neck. Connor was found lying on top of Duggy's body weeping as he embraced his dead brother, saying: "I'm so sorry, Duggy, this is all my fault," by the policemen and ambulance driver an hour after Douglas Avery McEvoy passed away.

Connor McEvoy was taken in for questioning following the freak accident, which to the police, seemed a lot more like manslaughter. Statements from the fellow partygoers did not help his case. Nor did statements from the bartender in Stanning. Connor was drug-tested and of course tested positive for cocaine.

As for the door that led to nowhere, it was said the homeowners were working on installing a balcony and had only gotten as far as framing the doorway and hanging the door. Everybody at the house-party but Connor and Duggy had known about it. They had also made up stories of witnessing Connor (most of them actually said Robby) push his brother out of the door because they knew their friend's parents were in some deep shit for not having it boarded shut. They had thought that if they could make it seem like foul play, and also make them believe Connor had brought the cocaine to their innocent little house party; the police would just forgive the homeowners and this ugly nightmare could be put behind them.

Since the door hadn't been boarded shut in accordance with OSHA regulations, his court-appointed attorney had told him he may get lucky and be convicted of Involuntary Manslaughter, and he'd only have to serve up to a maximum of five years in prison. But as the false testimonies poured in, the attorney's face began to have an obvious look of skepticism.

The police, as well as his attorney, had tried multiple times to reach his mother in Indiana and his father that supposedly lived in Iowa, but only got a busy tone for both every time.

Luckily, bail was set for $5,000 and Connor was released due to a man named Stuart Barkens paying it in full.

It was awful nice of Stu-Dog to help out one of Valerie's sons, but Connor would have much rather remained in jail than to walk the very ground he used to walk with his brother, Duggy. This had all only happened in the span of a week. If Duggy had remained alive they would've been in Garrisville with their little brother, surprising him for his birthday.

Upon his release, on the 16th of August; one day before Robby's birthday, Connor couldn't take much more of what had been handed to him.

Connor Jay McEvoy (whose nickname could've very well been CJ had he not made it clear to everyone to not call him CJ) had asked Stu-Dog to give him a ride to his father's house. There was of course no way of knowing that William McEvoy had become Big Bad Bill from the House Upon the Hill after slaying the pedophilic dragon that had haunted his youngest son's dreams. As far as Connor knew, he'd be walking into a bible-thumping William's house, where he apparently no longer believed in phone lines. The truth had turned out to be much worse.

Connor and Stu-Dog arrived at William McEvoy's house an hour after being released from jail. It was only 10:00 in the morning, yet Connor's expected friendly welcome home had been replaced by bullets whizzing past his head. It wasn't until Connor bravely exited the vehicle that Big Bad Bill stopped firing his rifle. Luckily, William's accuracy was amiss thanks to the alcohol.

At first Connor thought his father's house had been taken over by a white-haired madman. When he realized the white-haired madman was in fact his father; Connor almost forgot about his current situation and his pending prison time.

"Woah, woah, woah, woah!" yelled William to himself as he realized the car that had stopped on his property was *NOT* a masturbating caveman but his son, Connor (*or is that Robby? Looks like Robby with a shitty little mustache*).

William had been on quite the bender since murdering Richard Warmurt in cold blood; and hadn't had *ANY* visitors since. Which is extremely lucky for anyone out cruising around because this white-haired madman may have killed them for no reason. "Fucker almost killed me," Connor said aloud to himself.

Stu-Dog was long gone after Connor left his Pontiac Sunfire. Stu-Dog's Sunfire had actually been red instead of silver, but Richard Warmurt's silver Sunfire had turned red that dark day. And then it had been burned from history, but unfortunately, not memory. Not for Big Bad Bill.

William McEvoy was even drunker than Duggy and Connor on their last night together.

Connor yelled "Woah!" just as his father was yelling the same thing to himself.

When all was somewhat calm, Connor told his father that Douglas died.

Like dead, died. Like never coming back, died.

Connor began to cry hysterically trying to tell his father this terrible news; he hadn't said it out loud until now. The cops sure said it over and over but he himself hadn't.

William couldn't seem to grasp the idea. He kept mumbling about how he owns this house now and how he really just needs to go get Robby from Indiana but doesn't know his current location and when he drunkenly asked the operator for a Robert McEvoy in Indiana and only got a smartass response, he threw his cordless phone across the room, shattering it to pieces.

Connor was then hit with an awful feeling that he wished he'd never felt:

That all of what has happened with the family is Robby's fault. Him and Duggy would be perfectly fine right now had they not had the idea to go see their little brother. Their father would be in *WAY* better shape had Robby not left him behind. Which led to another thought:

What's Mom been having to put up with in Indiana, where Robby can't stop suckling on her teat for one day? Is she as dead as Duggy?

His awful thoughts were then escalated to hearing himself say: *How bout we go the fuck UPTHTAIRTH? Take me to your Master,* and *Thank you, Robby!*

Hadn't Connor been the one to carry Duggy halfway up to his terrible death?

Hadn't Connor been the one that selfishly just wanted cocaine?

Hadn't Connor been the one to lose focus on his best friend while he snorted more lines than was offered to him? While everyone else was making it clear something terrible had happened?

What if I hadn't done that line of coke and stopped him from opening that door?

Could I have saved him?

What if I hadn't made him go upstairs in the first place?

What if I hadn't decided to play hooky and we just went to work instead? What if… What if… WHAT IF???

When William McEvoy announced he was going to bed at 6:00 in the evening, Connor's "what ifs" drove him to sneak his father's rifle up to the attic. The AR10 had been resting against the couch all day long. He could almost hear the rifle asking him to take it away from William forever, and when he finally heard his father snoring ignorantly at 6:30, he opened the door to William's bedroom and whispered, "I'm sorry, Daddy. I'll be up in the attic." Connor Jay McEvoy then went upstairs, zipped himself head-first into a heavy-duty sleeping bag, and shot himself with his father's gun atop Robby's old mattress.

Chapter 11
We Gotta Get Out of This Place

As previously mentioned, Kurtis Harper had told a few tales to elaborate on how the attic had become haunted. Robert could never tell which stories to believe and kept in the back of his mind that they could *ALL* turn out to be total bullshit. But what *anyone* would have a hard time believing, especially if they knew how drastically his schizophrenia had escalated in the past three years; is that the only story he truly ever *made up* was the nightmare story of the Soul Reaver. He used it to put Robert's mind at ease and was hoping to be forgiven for his random blackouts. All his other far-fetched stories were indeed cold hard truth.

There was one story Kurtis really wanted to tell Robert, but his evil friends upstairs were persuading him to never tell anyone. They must've finally killed his only nice friend, Keith, because he hasn't heard from him in almost two weeks. Or maybe he just *IS* Keith now. He really can't tell. All he knows for sure is that he seems to be in control of himself and has been able to ignore his evil friends without feeling hypnotized or distracted by them. He wants to tell Robert *EVERYTHING*.

He wants to tell him how his best friend, Jeremy Knight, had turned out to be the reason he got jumped by the Vice Lords. Jeremy had complained to his cousin the day after the Coffman house incident about how hard Kurtis had punched him in the balls. He never meant for any harm to come to Kurtis, he was only joking about it and was planning on scheduling a Rockwar so they could just hash it out that way. But Jeremy Knight's cousin had made some plans of his own and was involved in the jumping.

He was the one with the bat.

And he's also the one Kurtis will never seek revenge on out of respect for his old pal, Jeremy.

Kurtis had obtained this information from a strange couple who started hanging around outside his house that in fact turned out to be Andrew Wallabee Pfister and Nurse Becca Beckins.

Before the deadly duo disappeared into hiding from their exposed operation; Mister Fister decided to hang around his ex-girlfriend's house. Becca had told him that the young boy living in Jennifer's old home had been jumped thanks to his best friend, and Andy loved such stories of betrayal. He himself was the posterchild of Best Friend.

How did she know this information, you may wonder?

Well, when she wasn't murdering old men and eviscerating their genitalia, she was volunteering in a program designed to help kids struggling in the ghetto.

She took a young boy named Jeremy out for ice cream and listened to him cry about how it was all his fault his friend got jumped and couldn't tell the police or his parents but *HAD* to tell somebody. Nurse Becca told the young boy his secret was safe with her.

Kurtis was not angry with his friend having heard this new information. Not until he started having very bad dreams, which had come to him in the wake of Andy Pfister and his ugly girlfriend. They smelled of dead bodies and unbathed shit-chutes, and their very presence made his skin crawl. He could *feel* them for hours after they left. It was almost as if they had died in his bedroom and haunted him with unspeakable demons. The bad dreams seemed to have awakened something in him. It was around this time the voices in his head began to speak and from then on, he pretended Jeremy Knight didn't exist. A year after the Coffman house incident, Jeremy and his family escaped the clutches of Garrisville and moved west to Arizona. He wanted to tell Robert all of this because he had let his mental infestation ruin an awesome friendship back in '97 and it appeared to be trying the same thing all over again.

He wanted to tell Robert the truth about his brothers' phone calls and that the Soul Reaver was just a video game he had once played on his buddy's Sega Dreamcast. Although they were definitely going to have to explore why Robert had seen a black hole. That was something Kurtis could never explain, and he was honestly a little freaked out about it.

His head was screaming at him for even thinking of such rebellion to the point Kurtis had a splitting headache and was forced to lay down and sleep for a while. Actually, it wasn't just for a while, Kurtis had ended up sleeping for three days straight. His dreams were greatly infected with vivid imaging of Robert's entire family falling apart. He had known what Douglas and Connor looked like (*and also sounded and talked like*) upon seeing the Golden Day photo on Robby's night-table. He had no real way of knowing what William could actually look like, but the white-haired man of his Neverland bared almost identical resemblance to Douglas. Kurtis played the part of scared little Robby in these dreams while discovering terrible truths perhaps better left untouched. He seemed to have found a new level of sleep much deeper than REM.

However, the evil within him had no problem controlling his physical body while he was in his fever-driven slumber. He had slept-walked to his phone and done his pick-up hang-up routine as the Police Department in Stanning was calling to notify Valerie her middle child was dead, and her eldest child was in jail. If he hadn't fallen into what seemed like a coma, he'd be pouring his heart out to Robert and begging for forgiveness; hopefully ending his mental war once and for all. But so far, his evil friends were winning.

When he finally awoke, he was in excruciating pain. It felt as though he had run a marathon in his sleep. He was highly dehydrated and malnourished but was neither hungry nor thirsty. He laid awake in his bed with his thoughts for a few more days, making random appearances downstairs for a piss or more iced water. At one point Christy had stopped him halfway up the stairs and begged him to go with her to see a doctor. Kurtis had then surprised her with a long hug. They both cried heavily and happily as they embraced each other, neither of them knowing why, but both able to guess it was for everything they had been through together. They said their I Love You's, and Christy was relieved to feel that Kurtis wasn't burning up with fever. She watched him walk the rest of the way up the stairs with a smile that hadn't touched her face since their family was whole. She was overwhelmed with a great feeling that everything was going to be okay, something she hadn't felt since even long before Keith had left.

Kurtis was bound and determined to get better. Not just better from the sudden slight sickness he was fighting, but his mental health was going to be fixed whether those assholes in the attic liked it or not. He was going to apologize to Robert as initially planned; be a better brother to both him and Tabitha; continue making his mother feel loved; and most importantly make sure what's left of his family doesn't get torn apart like something he had witnessed in his strange coma dreams. This, unfortunately, was Kurtis Harper's last shred of sanity; or perhaps better-worded: the very last piece of his actual self.

Robby has been in high spirits regardless of his bad dreams, which seem to be abandoning him at a quick rate. He can wake himself up out of these mind-horrors now and fall back asleep to far better, hip-hop driven dreams. His Walkman remains warm to the touch from repeatedly spinning and he knows he will soon need a new one. He has already cleaned the crystal eye with rubbing alcohol four times and lately it's acting as though the Play button is broken. He keeps his headphones on in his sleep and the bad dreams make appearance when his **Happy Birthday Bro! 2003 Mix!** Reaches its end. His future Walkman will most definitely have the Repeat-All function.

This music has been changing Robert McEvoy's entire perspective on life.

If he had ever thought to ask his brothers for their home address, he would certainly send them a heart-filled Thank You letter. He has called their house over a dozen times in the past week but all he gets for answer is an automated voicemail woman letting him know that the mailbox is currently full and to press 5 to go fuck himself. He can only assume they've moved away.

Doesn't really matter, his brothers are with him through this music. Both the CDs and the letter have embodied their very beings; they fill him with happy tears and provide light at the end of his tunnel. After extensive contemplation, he has decided to show *ALL* of his new birthday present to his mother in hopes she will take him back to Iowa. Back home. Back with Dig-Dug and Condor.

He figures the letter will be a sort of wake-up call for Valerie. That's sure what it was for him. He can envision her now, weeping happily but not without the stinging sorrow for leaving, as he himself had done; and saying something like: *Ok, Robby. Let's go home.*

He just has to wait a couple more hours for her to get home from work.

Valerie had quit the stripping gig *AND* the drinking. She apologized in advance to Christy that they would have less money with her previous waitress job and Christy said either way it wouldn't matter. They were already several months ahead on rent and the daycare on its own right now could take care of all other due payments. She reassured Valerie this was a vital step for her and Robby's relationship; for a child could never grow to respect his mother if she's out sleeping around all the time and private dancing for money, any old music will do. The drinking was the first to stop, because Valerie had ridiculously been paranoid of not putting in an honest two weeks' notice at the She Club. Christy had made fun of her for an entire fourteen days.

Both vices had been easy enough to rid herself of, surprisingly. It may sound funny, but she was indeed as addicted to stripping as she was to alcohol. She hadn't displayed any withdrawal symptoms and was apparently so moved by her own will that she was naturally high on life and happier than she had been in a while. Robby's birthday present from Duggy arrived a week before his actual birthday and it couldn't have arrived at a better time. Valerie's mood and newfound self-respect seemed to Robby that she'd be more willing to do the right thing and head back north.

What he didn't realize was that Valerie had recently developed a nasal fixation. Everybody else in the house (excluding Kurtis), unbeknownst to Robby, had been growing suspicious over the past few days of her constant sniffle and fast talking. Her verbal diarrhea lately has grown from moderate to explosive. Robby, blinded by his own current enlightenment, just sees it as happy.

She started craving the once foreign drug to her out of nowhere about a week ago when she met a man named Alexander who claimed to hail from Ft. Lazarus, Florida and was just about to head back down there soon. He had jokingly asked her to come along, and she had jokingly answered, *Yes of course, just let me drop everything and I'll be on my way, Ha-ha!*

How was she to know he actually hailed from Everywhere, USA?

Or, how he had just swung through Iowa not too long ago and destroyed two lives of some poor young souls by bringing cocaine to a house-party, and is currently hitting the road on chance the feds up north find out the truth of that terrible night.

Two hours later, when Valerie's home and slightly wound down; is when she'll get the phone call that'll change the course of their lives, yet again, because Kurtis's entourage had allowed this particular 712 number to be answered by someone other than *them*.

When Big Bad Bill from the house upon the hill caught a glimpse of himself in the bathroom mirror for the first time in weeks; he jumped back in terror and fell ass-first into his claw-footed bathtub. He landed luckily without smacking his head on the lip of it and was completely un-harmed, but still extremely scared. What appeared to be left of William McEvoy in that awful glass reflection looked to have only a couple of years left before taking a dirt nap. What he saw was a drunken- and sunken-eyed white-haired lunatic who could easily pass an audition for a lead role in a movie about mad scientists suffering from radiation poisoning.

It wasn't a good look.

The nightmares he had been having since committing his first murder had suddenly seemed to be the ugly truth. He doesn't know his eldest son is still wrapped up in his cushioned coffin upstairs, and he has not noticed the Colt's disappearance from the couch, nor does he remember Connor ever being there whatsoever. The door was shut to the attic and there was no reason to even think of it.

In fact, the *only* thing he can think of now is his frightening appearance and bad dreams.

When the sandman paid visits to William McEvoy, which until recently had been few and far between; the dream-giver did so in a hostile fashion. He began wetting the bed, but every morning would blame the liquor for his wet sheets. The dreams were also what had been whiting his hair and thinning it into a frizzy, electrical-shocked look. The amount of stress he's endured while viewing his most recent mind-movies is staggering. He could only vaguely remember them at random when hit with a Deja-Vu moment that would stop him in his tracks.

A few things he knew for sure of them was that they were based in the future and Robby was living back upstairs and William was somehow in his seventies.

They had put the father-son relationship behind them and lived together as good friends. Maybe even Best friends.

Robby was about ten years older and was trying still to grow a mustache but failing. What he had on his upper lip instead looked more like a cat's whiskers.

And then some kind of outer-worldly altercation would occur that ended with Robby dead in the attic.

He was still sitting in his bathtub when the words "In the attic" began to swim circles inside his mind. His bathtub suddenly felt like a boat bobbing and twirling through a hurricane-driven sea. He then vomited last night's midnight snack (a 750ml bottle of Jim Beam) onto the tub's floor beside him and fell asleep.

This particular sleep was thankfully dreamless; it was more of a 15-minute power nap, and when he woke up and struggled himself out of the tub, he decided to check out the attic, but not before examining himself a little further in the mirror. No part of him remembering today is Robert's birthday.

The voices. They flooded in with their sinister conversations upon returning to his room after hugging his mother on the stairs. His exhaustion still heavy from oversleeping as he attempts to respond to them:

No.

Why not? Put them out of their misery. You saw what happened to the rest of the family. Kill them both. Get your life back. How can you focus on your family with these shitheads hanging around?

He's my friend. My brother. His mom's finally trying to get her shit together.

Oh, his lovely mother, yes. But you still hate *her, don't you? Either* you *kill the slut and her son, and* we'll *dispose of the bodies or vice-versa. What's left of Kurtis Harper is weak. It wouldn't be very hard.*

We'd be doing them a favor. Don't resist us.

The more you resist, the less you'll exist.

How many of you are there, now?

Does it really matter? Pay attention or blackout forever.

The argument continued as the phone rang. Nobody in the attic took notice.

Robby had been writing a rap song for the first time in months when Valerie came into the bedroom. He was sitting upright in his bed, headphones blaring, writing rapidly in his notebook. When he finally looked up as if he were stumped on a word and saw his mom, he jumped out of bed and hugged her tightly. She hugged back.

It had been a great week.

(For the upcoming schoolyear, Robby will be homeschooled by Valerie and will no longer have to suffer the tiresome labor of "fitting in." Last year had ended badly in the School for Pussies. There was no bullying this time around; he had just been ready to make friends and get himself a girlfriend and it just wasn't happening. Everybody there looked at him like an alien, including the teachers. Constantly ignored and never called upon by anyone for anything. He sat alone in the lunchroom. Even if he were to meet a nice girl, there was no way in Hell he'd be able to talk to her properly. The bad dreams had turned him into a stranger even *he* didn't know in the mirror. He felt that if he were to go back to Iowa, his brothers wouldn't recognize him either. His sense of humor had diminished and all that was left was an awkward robot on autopilot. There was just enough of himself to know that he was not happy. The bullying was somehow better. At least then he was noticed. His report card read **F** up and down and side to side. A note at the bottom of the final report had read *Have you ever considered homeschooling your child?* Turns out Valerie actually had considered it. That's when she decided to have one more Summer of Fun before the next schoolyear started so she could sober up and teach Robby from the homeschooling kit. And while she had her Summer of Fun, he had his Summer of Hell. It wasn't how he had begun watching the daycare kids every day so Christy could sit and "quietly" finger herself in her bedroom while looking at her cock-infested webcam feed. *Two in the butter, one in the gutter.* It wasn't that he hated watching the kids. He had actually grown to love the kids and it was over that summer that Robby decided he wanted to be a father someday. It wasn't how badly his dreams were recurring or how he started wetting the bed again, at random. It was Kurtis Harper. Robby couldn't quite place it, but he knew his strange new older brother was up to something bad. It was his devious grin and horrible attitude that ruined Robby's summer. There had been a week where Kurtis kept making fun of a little boy named Demetrius, one of the daycare kids. Demetrius was a two-year-old boy whose father was a black man and mother a white woman. Robert hadn't ever heard Kurtis use the N-word nor did he think Kurtis had a racist bone in his body until Demetrius and his family came around. Apparently seeing a black man with a white woman enraged him. Demetrius's parents would leave, and Kurtis would say something like: "Stupid fuckin broad! She's probably only with him for his giant jigaboo dick!" or "Mom, are they paying you double to watch this little niglet? Because they damn-well fucking should be!" Robert barely noticed how Kurtis's voice would change during these rants and he would think: *Say that in front of his father, you ignorant prick! I bet he'd kick your cracker-ass back to the stone age!* He loved Demetrius. He'd watch him chase the ginger twins around the house bow-legged yelling gibberish that only made sense to himself. Then the little guy would run up to *Wobby*—his gibberish didn't keep him from trying to say Robby—and give him a big hug and yell "Huggies!" Dude was a snuggler. It was impossible for Robert not to love Demetrius. He was a dark-skinned, chubby-cheeked, droopy-drawered, chunker-munker with the beginnings of a bitchin' afro. Robert was convinced it was impossible for *ANYONE* to not love Demetrius. That is until Kurtis Harper stormed down the stairs one day, pissed off from all the noise Robby and the kids were making, and spat in the little boy's face. Robert's ever-growing fear of Kurtis was quickly replaced with hot-blooded adrenaline…

"Man, are you fucking *KIDDING ME?!*" Robert yelled as he charged after Kurtis.

"Oh, how I've waited for this," said Kurtis calmly. The devious grin at full capacity.

Before Robby could even make a swing on his young, stupid vendetta toward a man twice his size; Kurtis wrapped his arm around the back of his neck and threw him effortlessly to the floor. The force of the throw led Robby face-first to the carpet, ringing his bell. When he opened his eyes all he saw was a flashing blue star like the Star of Life on the sides of ambulance trucks. He was already done fighting, but Kurtis was just beginning. He dropped onto Robby with all his 300-pound weight, driving his knee into the little fucker's back.

"What were your plans, BJ? Huh? Did you really think you could fuck with me?"

Robert did not reply. Could not reply. His face was too busy being shoved into the un-vacuumed carpet of the living room floor in front of *ALL* the daycare kids. He was able to notice, however, that Kurtis's voice had changed. It almost sounded British. A proper evil voice if ever there was one. And it was a good thing his vision was currently too occupied with fuzzies and blue stars, because Kurtis's eyes had become a shark's eyes; and his beet-red face trembled and shook as rapidly as one of Christy's vibrators on Squirt Mode. He looked like the devil. The daycare kids, including

Demetrius, ran away in terror at the sight of his ghastly transformation.

"This is it, BJ!" Snot running down Kurtis's nose, tears streaking his cheeks.

"This is the end, beautiful…" He suddenly stopped. Kurtis Harper was Kurtis Harper again.

He stood up immediately once realizing what he was doing and was horrified at how out of control this particular blackout had gotten. This was by far the worst. He helped Robby to his feet, apologizing, begging for forgiveness. Robert McEvoy gained his vision back, adrenaline working through his body yet again; only this time he was smart enough not to tempt the awful British man out of hiding, and ran out of the house, slamming the door behind him. His clenched fist found the nearest tree and found it hard. He broke his pinky knuckle on impact and screamed aloud; the only witness was the smiling sun across the street. The one that seemed to frown as you turned away. Sunny Bread's odd mascot was really the only sun in Garrisville. The constant smog, thick and gray, gave zero visibility to the sky above. But that fucking smile of that sun was always visible! A crazy smile that seemed to warn you: *Go back inside and lock up tight, there ain't anything out here for you.* And that's what his summer became. Evil smiling sun outside; evil smiling Kurtis inside.)

But this last week had been a great one.

Kurtis had been up in his room doing God knows what for most of it.

The CDs from his brothers have been helping him regain his sanity/happiness.

And today's his birthday!

"Happy Birthday, Sweetie Pie!" says Valerie as they hug each other. "I got you something I think you'll really love! It's out in the kitchen. I was gonna have you open it in front of everybody, but everybody seems to be in their bedrooms. I'm gonna go get it. You wait here."

Robby was so caught up in his plan to talk to her about going back to Iowa that he had forgotten all about presents! *Please be an X-Box,* he hopes.

Just as Valerie walks into the kitchen, the phone rings.

Upstairs in the attic, Kurtis is trying his hardest to ward off his evil friends.

Robby heard the phone ring from the bedroom, heard his mom shout a little bit. Whether it was an angry shout or a friendly shout, he didn't know. A few minutes later his mom gives him an X-Box for his birthday. She looks tired, claims today was a long day, and that she must nap for a little while.

Kurtis is still doing an okay job of keeping his roommates at bay.

William McEvoy is once and for all questing toward Indiana. The sleeping bag in the attic had quickly decided him.

He's carrying Connor's TracFone (that's how he got ahold of that stupid bitch) that he in fact believes to be Robby's.

Because that's who was in the sleeping bag.

Valerie McEvoy is pretending to sleep, wondering how she's going to get Robby to go to Florida with her. She knows her ex-husband is coming for her.

Robert McEvoy is happily utilizing his new present; playing the game that came with his X-Box. A game called *The Legacy of Kain: Blood Omen II*. The back of the case says it's some sort of sequel to the game *Soul Reaver*. Seeing the words in print rather than imagining a buzzing black hole was still a bit unsettling; but he finally has the X-Box!

No time to worry about what this might mean for his nightmares.

He played his X-Box until midnight and dozed off with the game still going, controller in hand. He had forgotten to talk to his mom about going back to Iowa.

That was okay, though. There was always tomorrow.

Valerie had dozed off at some point and awoke at 3A.M. to see her son sleeping and immediately thought of the perfect plan.

At 3:45 both Valerie and Robby are in their Isuzu Rodeo with most of their stuff; excluding anything that was in the attic, packed into the hatchback. They are going back to Iowa…

…Supposedly.

Whatever Kurtis's posse had in store for them they will never know.

But at roughly 4:30 in the morning, Kurtis Harper finally loses his mental war and blacks out for the last time.